WINNER TAKES ALL

SUSAN HAYES

Winner Takes All

First Print Publication: July 2021

Cover Design: Mina Carter

Editor: Amanda Brown

Published by: Black Scroll Publications Ltd.

DEDICATION

For my Mum and Dad, for all their love and support.

ABOUT THE BOOK

Never again. That's the promise she made to herself after two men broke her heart… but is it a promise she should keep?

Phylomenia only has two rules. Never profit from someone else's suffering, and don't make the same mistake twice. Rekindling the flames of a thirty-year old love affair would mean repeating the biggest mistake of her life—falling in love with Scott and Garrett. So why is she tempted to fall again?

Scott made a mistake that cost him everyone he loved. The time has come to make things right.

Duty. Loyalty. Honor. Scott Archer built his life around those principles. But duty is a cold companion, and honor can't heal the scars of the past. When fate brings the three of them together again, Scott must reforge the links between them or risk losing his loves forever.

Garrett never expected to see them again. The one that got away...and the one that never was.

Decades ago their love was torn apart by lies, death, and secrets. Now Garrett has both of them back in his sights, and he's determined to rebuild what they once had... only better. Phyomenia and Scott aren't same people they were back then, and neither is he. He knows what he wants, and he's going to take it, any way he can.

Old flames. New dangers. And one last chance to make a play for love... Winner takes all.

PROLOGUE

OUT ON THE EDGE OF CIVILIZED SPACE IS A RAG-TAG collection of space stations and platforms known as the Drift. It's a haven for the hunted, the lost, and those seeking second chances. The people who live there hail from every species, class, and corner of the galaxy, but they all have one thing in common: they don't belong anywhere else.

There's nothing beyond the Drift but wild space and an asteroid belt full of ore-rich rocks. The asteroids are mined by hundreds of vessels and their hard-working crews. When the ships deliver their haul to be processed, those crews hit the infamous bars, casinos, and pleasure houses that are the Drift's primary source of income...and only source of entertainment.

It's a world of its own. One where corporations

rule, the laws are flexible, and everything is for sale, for the right price.

Welcome to the Drift.

1

So this was the infamous Nova Club—the home base of the cyborgs that had managed to uncover some of the galaxy's largest corporations' greatest secrets and triggered a public reckoning that had changed the rules of the game.

Garrett Michaels took in every detail of the place as he moved through the crowd. The décor was blue and silver, decidedly different from the more strident color schemes usually found in places like this. The bar itself was a gleaming stretch of metal that spanned most of one wall. It was manned by several bartenders, all living, breathing beings instead of servo-droids. In fact, none of the usual bots and droids anywhere to be seen—also unusual.

Staff were serving drinks and taking orders, with more of them supervising the gaming area. They weren't all cyborgs, either, a fact that surprised him. His reports indicated the owners were a distrustful lot who kept very much to themselves.

He'd been here less than five minutes, yet it was clear his reports were wrong. He counted several Pherans and Torskis on staff as well as some ordinary humans, all wearing clothing marked with the club's logo.

It didn't bode well for the rest of his intelligence if they'd managed to get even that basic fact wrong. He was going to have to double check everything. Bad intel led to unpleasant outcomes. He knew that better than most, and he was being paid a small fortune to make sure that whatever happened over the next few weeks, his clients would not experience a repeat of what happened the last time they'd come to Astek for business. Bellex Shipbuilding had lost a private ship, much of her crew, and a senior representative to a cyborg assassin who had left a trail of dead bodies in her wake.

That wouldn't happen this time—at least, not to *his* client. The others would have to rely on their own security advisors and the protection of the Interstellar Armed Forces that seemed to be everywhere on Astek station. Scott Archer had apparently learned from his last mistake.

It was strange to think he was breathing the same air as Archer again after all these years. Thirty. *Veth.* Had it really been thirty years since they'd last seen each other? When had he gotten old enough for that to be possible?

He was still musing the passage of time when he spotted her. At first, he was sure his mind was playing tricks on him. *She* couldn't be here. The woman watching him from across the room had to be a stranger, and his memory was just painting her in a familiar light. Phylomenia Harrington could not be here.

Then she scowled, and for a moment it was like the gravity tripled and then vanished, leaving him floating.

It *was* her.

She glared at him with clear recognition, her expression so stormy he wouldn't have been surprised to be struck by lightning in the next few seconds.

He was on his way to her before he was even aware he was moving, a careful smile hiding the turmoil he felt. Of all the bars in all the backwater worlds and stations... what the hell was she doing in this one?

She handed off a child to one of the other females at her table and got to her feet. Her hair had silvered, but she still moved with that same long-legged grace that had drawn him to her the first night they'd met. Was the baby hers? Her granddaughter, maybe?

Jealousy tore through him at the thought of her being with someone else. It was selfish and irrational. They'd parted ways thirty years ago, but he'd allowed himself to indulge in the fantasy that Phylomenia had never moved on. That she was out there somewhere, waiting for the day they met again.

Apparently, today was that day.

He ran through several opening lines on the way to meet her. Flattery wouldn't work. Apologizing put him at a disadvantage from the start. He had settled on a simple declaration of surprise to see her, but he never got a chance to use it. The moment he was in earshot, she set a hand on her hip and fixed him with a steely stare.

"Garrett Michaels. What the *fraxx* are you doing here?"

Her words came out with that poured-honey drawl he'd loved back then, though a hint of frost in her tone made him wary. "Hello, Mena."

"No. No one calls me that anymore. My friends call me Phyl." She arched a silver brow. "You can call me Captain Harrington. Now, I'll ask you again, what are you doing here?"

He couldn't help himself. He grinned. "You haven't changed a bit."

The lines around her mouth deepened as a ghost of a smile touched her lips. "Neither have you. You're still a stubborn son of a starbeast who won't answer a simple question."

"Me? I'm here on business. Security for the gala coming up. You? To be honest, this is the last place in the galaxy I expected to find you, given..." He didn't dare to utter Scott Archer's name until he had a better grasp of what was going on. Two cyborgs stood nearby, clearly keeping an eye on him. They were identical, and unless his researchers had *fraxxed* up that intel, too, he knew exactly who they were. Their names were Vic and Ward, and they were recently retired assassins.

"I live here."

He wasn't sure how she made that simple statement into a challenge, but somehow she did. "You do?"

Phyl nodded once. Her expression was chilly, but he caught a twinkle in her steel-blue eyes. The spitfire was enjoying this.

"I do." She inclined her head toward the table she'd been seated at earlier. "That's my family up there."

"And here," one of the towering twins of doom took a half-step closer while the other drew a slender Pheran female behind him.

Garrett ignored the posturing and focused on Phylomenia. "Family? You found someone crazy enough to take you on full time?"

The moment the words left his mouth, he knew he'd *fraxxed* up. All the light left her eyes and he had to fight the urge to take a step back. He knew that look, and thirty years had only sharpened the edges of her anger.

"Just because you walked away, you think no one else would want me?"

"I didn't walk away."

Phyl scoffed. "My mistake. You *ran*."

"Dammit, Mena. That's not what happened and you know it."

"That's exactly what happened! I went to see you that night and was told your transfer had already gone through. You were gone, Garrett. Without a word. Not even a damned note. I deserved better."

"You did. But I left you a message."

"I never got it."

Anger tore through him. "Scott never told you?"

"We weren't speaking. Remember?" she shot back.

"Phyl?" One of the cyborgs touched her shoulder lightly. "Want us to remove him? We're happy to do it."

"More than happy to," the other one chimed in.

"Tempting, but no. Not yet." She offered the cyborgs a sweet smile. "But thank you for the offer."

She turned back to him and the smile vanished. "You. Me. Talk. Now."

"Fine, I'll buy you a drink and we can—"

"No." She pointed to a door by the bar. "With me. Boys, tell Kit and Luke I'm borrowing the gym for a bit. It's soundproofed."

"Why do we need soundproofing?" he asked, falling in beside her as Phylomenia made her way toward the door.

"Because I don't want the sprites to hear the very bad language I'm about to use. Those are my grandbabies, and I will protect them from anything bad in this universe, including me."

Grandchildren. Jealousy sizzled in his veins at the

idea of her building a life without him. She'd never gotten his message. Never known... *Fraxx*.

"I'm going to kill him."

She didn't even ask who he was talking about. "Get in line."

Phylomenia's brain was going in circles at close to light speed. Garrett was here. Worse. Garrett was here and she was intentionally seeking out a private place for them to talk.

Talk. She laughed at herself. The man was still sex on a stick and annoying as hell. Either she was going to smack him, yell at him, or kiss him until the last thirty years were banished from both their memories. Right now, she had no idea which one would happen. Hell, maybe all three... and wouldn't that just be a *fraxxing* mess to fix later.

"Tell me he doesn't know you're here." She glanced over to Garrett. He was keeping pace with her easily. She was tall for a woman, but he was taller—bigger in every way. Long legs, broad shoulders, and while silver streaked his beard and his temples, he was still the bear of a man she'd fallen for all those years ago.

"We don't speak. If he knows, it's only because he's got his nose stuck into places it doesn't belong."

"Then there's a chance he knows. That man likes

to think he knows everything that goes on in his little kingdom."

"Is that what this is? I thought Astek owned this station."

"They do. But until he gets his new..." she cut herself off before revealing information that wasn't hers to share. "Astek is more or less a military base right now, and he's the senior officer out here."

"Phyl!"

She recognized Kit's voice and turned around. "Hey, Kit. Did the boys tell you I need to borrow the gym?"

The big cyborg folded his arms across his chest and glowered at Garrett. "They did. And you know you can use any place you need. A private meeting room might be more comfortable, though."

"The gym would be better."

He eyed her for a moment and then nodded. "I'll be right outside."

"You own the bar, sweetie. You're too busy to play bouncer."

"Family first."

Garrett's eyes widened slightly. "He's your family, too?"

Feeling utterly wicked, she mustered her sunniest smile and touched a hand to her cheek. "Oh dear, where are my manners? Garrett Michaels, meet Kit Armas, one of the club's owners and my son-in-law." It wasn't exactly true, of course. Zura wasn't her daughter by any traditional definition, but she was as close to one as Phyl would ever have. She was family.

Kit didn't blink at his new title. "Mr. Michaels. Welcome to the Nova Club. Enjoy your stay, and if you upset Phylomenia, they will never find your body. Clear?"

"I appreciate a man who cuts straight to the point, Mr. Armas. I'll keep your warning in mind."

It should not have impressed her that he stood toe to toe with Kit without blinking. Nor should she have taken the time to notice that he was almost as big and well-built as the strapping cyborg. She really needed to get it together. The coming conversation needed to be about burying the past, not starting another chapter.

"Did someone let Archer know I want to talk to him?"

"The message was conveyed. Apparently he's on his way." Kit sounded amused, and she wished she'd been there to hear that little exchange.

Garrett made a soft sound of surprise. "You summoned Scott? I thought you said he ran this kingdom?"

"He does. But I still outrank him. I was here first."

Kit walked them down to the gym and waved them through the main door. "I'll be here if you need me."

"I can handle him," she told Kit and winked as she stepped through the door.

Weights and cardio equipment filled most of the space inside. Grav-plates had been installed under the floor, making it easy to increase the intensity of a workout by ramping up the gravity. She made her way to the sparring mats, taking off her boots before stepping onto the floor.

"Seriously?" Garrett asked. "I thought we were here to talk."

"I like having options."

"If it comes to a fight, you know I'm going to win." He followed her, bending over to take off his shoes and giving her a nice view of a very well-tailored pair of pants hugging a toned ass.

She bounced on her toes a few times. "Last time we did this, I didn't have medi-bots. Don't let the gray hair fool you. I'm a nano-enhanced badass now."

He snapped upright and stared at her, mouth open. "You took the treatment? When? How? No one but the..." He groaned. "You're not just part of the Armas family. You're part of their *fraxxing* rebellion."

"Since the very beginning." After a lifetime of looking out for herself, she'd found a cause to fight for— a good one. Whereas Garrett had chosen another path. "I guess this puts us on different sides of this war."

Garrett stalked out onto the mat. "We're not at war."

"No? Then why is Tianna hosting a peace summit here soon? That's what it is, you know."

"Tianna? You're on a first name basis with Tianna Astor? *Fraxxing* hell, Mena, you really have upped your game since we last saw each other."

"She's my daughter-in-law. And don't call me that."

"Sorry, habit. I feel like I fell into a wormhole and woke up thirty years in the past."

"We'd both have a lot less gray if that was the truth. You should see Scotty. Almost pure silver now. He keeps trying to tell me it makes him look distinguished."

"How is it that you're so pissed at me that we're standing on a sparring mat, yet you still talk to Scott?" A look of something that might have been jealousy flashed in Garrett's eyes. "Please tell me you're not back with him."

"How the *fraxx* would that be any of your business? You walked out on me. On us."

"For the last time, I didn't walk out. I got tapped for a mission. Undercover. It was only supposed to be for six months. I was coming back, dammit."

"Bullshit. You quit your commission and went corporate. I checked. You signed on with Gigan Corp., the same assholes I'd sold my soul to."

"You're not listening. I didn't sign on. I was assigned. All of this was in the vid recording I left for you. And it's my business because if Scott never gave you that recording, I am going to remove that stick from his ass and beat him to death with it without wiping it down first."

"I'd forgotten how vulgar you were. No wife to polish off those rough edges?" She was baiting him on purpose. If he was yelling at her, she could stay mad at him instead of trying to figure out why she wanted him to be jealous of Scott, even though that was the last thing she needed in her life.

"No wife. And you haven't answered my question." He took two steps toward her, squaring his shoulders and giving her the same look he had the night they'd met. "Talk."

"Scott and I have managed to bury the proverbial hatchet, but no, I'm not with him. That man is more married to his job now than he was back then. Even if I wanted to, I wouldn't have a snowball's chance in a supernova of competing with his career.

She set her jaw and narrowed her eyes. It was a look she'd been told could scare the thorns off a Jeskyran. "There. I talked. Now it's your turn. You really expect me to believe that you were on an undercover mission? What happened when the six months were up? You decide your new life was more fun than the old one? More money? I know about you, Garrett Michaels. You always wanted money. Now, you've got more of it than you could spend in three lifetimes." Which was ironic, given that of the two of them, she was the one whose lifespan could now be measured in centuries, and she'd be working every year of it. Life might have given her a family and a place to call home, but all she had to her name was an aging ship and a bank account with a balance barely above zero.

"Yes, the money was good. The danger pay for that

initial mission alone was almost enough to pay off your debts. That's why I accepted, Mena. I was doing it for you."

Phylomenia closed the last bit of distance between them, jabbing a finger into the well-tailored front of his suit. "Don't you dare tell me you were going to pay off my debt. If that were true, why didn't you tell me yourself?"

"It's the truth."

"So you walked away from us to save me and never said a word?" She shook her head. "That doesn't make sense. Maybe it did back then, but that was a lifetime ago.

From where I stand, it's just a weak excuse for walking out on us."

"As I recall, Garrett wasn't the only one who walked away, Phyl." Scott joined the conversation. She'd been so intent on Garrett she hadn't heard the door open, and judging by the look on his face, neither had Garrett. It was the first time the three of them had been together since the night it had all gone to hell.

She turned, ready to argue that wasn't how it had happened, but Garrett didn't give her a chance.

"You son of a bitch!" The big lug charged Scott, hitting him hard enough he staggered back into a wall.

Phyl groaned. "Here we go again. Thirty years and nothing's changed."

It wasn't true, though. She wasn't the same person she'd been back then. She'd been young, ambitious, and fearless. She thought she had the galaxy by the tail and had stormed the stars with a recklessness that should have gotten her killed a dozen times over. She'd learned plenty since then, and some of the most painful lessons had been taught to her by the two men currently trading punches with each other.

That much was still the same. The only men she'd ever given her heart to still preferred to fight rather than talk to each other.

Men.

2

SCOTT ARCHER HAD BEEN OFF DUTY AND BACK IN his quarters just long enough to change out of his uniform and pour himself a drink before his comms chirped.

"One day, I'm going to get through an entire evening without an interruption." It was what he said every night. As far as he could remember, it had been ten or so years since the last time he'd accomplished that feat, but he kept hoping history would repeat itself.

A quick glance at the screen made him wince. Cynder Armas wouldn't call unless there was a problem they couldn't handle, and when a bunch of cyborgs couldn't deal with something... it generally wasn't an easy fix.

He accepted the incoming vid call. "Archer here. What exploded this time, Cynder?"

"No explosions yet, but you need to get down here. Now."

"What's going on?"

"Honestly? I have no idea. Phyl spotted a guy none of us had seen before. She growled and said that someone needed to let you know that if you knew he was here, she'd be coming for you next."

"Who?" he asked, already out of his chair.

"No idea. She asked if they could use the gym to talk. Mentioned soundproofing?" Cyn touched her hand to her screen, and a file uploaded to the view, temporarily replacing her face. "That's him."

He recognized the man immediately. What the *fraxx* was Michaels doing out here? And why didn't he have the survival instinct to avoid being alone with Phylomenia?

"I'll be right there. Is someone with her right now?"

"Outside the door. Why, is she in danger?"

"No. But he is. I'm on my way."

He dropped his comms into his pocket and made an undignified dash from his quarters to the Nova Club, not even bothering to stop at the security checkpoint set up where the IAF's assigned space met the public part of Astek Station.

Toro was on duty at the club's door. He saw Scott headed his way and opened the door for him without saying a word.

He'd been inside the club so often he knew the way blindfolded. He even had access to the employee areas since that was where the merry band of renegades he'd somehow inherited with this job usually met to plan their responses to whatever the universe had thrown at them. He'd been privy to more than a few of those planning sessions in his time here, and he'd learned two things about the Armas crew. They were dangerous adversaries, and they were more than a little insane. When he'd discovered Phylomenia was one of their number, he hadn't been the least bit surprised. They were her kind of people.

He'd figured out how to coexist with Phylomenia. It hadn't been easy, but they'd somehow found a way to get from awkwardly ignoring each other to something he hoped might be the beginning of a new chapter for the two of them. Nothing had been formalized yet. He was moving slowly. Just dinners and time spent together while rekindling the flames that used to burn between them. They still didn't speak of some topics, and they had a whole minefield full of memories neither of them wanted to revisit. If Garrett was back, it was a good bet they were all about to land in the middle of the minefield, and he was the only one who knew where some of the biggest bombs were buried.

His older sister had always warned him that keeping secrets would get him killed one day. Today she might be proven right.

Kit stood guard outside the gym door, his body

locked in the perfect stillness that only cyborgs could manage.

"All quiet?" Scott asked.

"Not really. Who is he?"

"A ghost from the past."

Kit just arched one brow. "He seemed pretty alive to me. For now."

"It would have been better for everyone if he'd stayed dead."

Kit snorted and slapped a hand over the door control. It slid open with barely a whisper and Scott stepped through just in time to hear Phyl challenging Garrett.

"From where I stand, it's just a weak excuse for walking out on us."

And just like that, the years vanished and he was a young lieutenant commander again, his career freshly launched into the stratosphere and his personal life nothing but a smoking crater.

"As I recall it, Garrett wasn't the only one who walked away, Phyl," he said. Scott had expected Phylomenia to push back. He was wrong. Garrett came at him like a rogue comet.

He hit the wall hard, and then the two of them were hammering at each other like they were back in their bar-brawling days. No refinement. No style. Just bashing and kicking, fists and insults flying fast.

"You still hit like a girl," he taunted Garrett.

"And you still can't land a punch to save your life."

"Thirty years and you still drop your left every time you move your feet."

"Three *fraxxing* decades and you're *still* an asshole."

Scott landed a kick that sent Garrett staggering sideways. "I'm not the one who tackled me the moment I walked through the *fraxxing* door."

"You never told her!" Garrett roared and charged again, his punches little more than wild haymakers.

He focused on blocking for a few seconds, but Garrett managed to get past his defenses and land a ringing blow that made Scott's vision fill with stars. He spat out a mouthful of blood and stepped back, giving himself a second to regroup.

"She left, you moron. I never saw her again. You both *left*!

"Bullshit. You're both here on this station. You could have told her any time you wanted to. Married or not, she deserved to know the truth."

"Married?" Why the hell did Garrett think she was married? As far as he knew, the only man Phylomenia was seeing socially was him.

"I didn't hit you that hard. Yes. Married. Grandkids. A family. At least she got a chance to do it right. Not like us."

Scott lashed out and caught Garrett in the midsection with one foot. "Speak for yourself. I did just fine, thank you!"

"Enough!" Phyl yelled, and the next thing he knew

he was on the floor with what felt like an army of invisible Torskis sitting on him.

"Wha?" Garrett muttered. He'd gone down about a meter away with his face pressed into the floor mat so hard his query came out as more of a muffled grunt.

Scott managed to get enough air into his lungs for a brief explanation. "Grav-plate."

"Fraxx."

"Are you two quite done proving that humans evolved from apes? I've seen silverback gorillas with better manners," Phyl said, her drawl was deeper than he'd heard it in years.

"They're extinct," Garrett pointed out.

"Don't argue with the only person in the room who can reach the grav-plate controls for this part of the gym."

"Sorry," Garrett muttered.

The number of invisible Torskis lessened and Scott sucked in a lungful of air. "Thank you."

"Don't thank me yet. The gravity stays at three until I get some answers."

He and Garrett both managed to turn themselves so they could see Phyl. She was standing just outside the effect of the grav-plate, hands on her hips, lips pressed together, and her eyes cool and narrowed.

"Tell her," Garrett growled.

"Why? Unless you have a time machine, it's not going to change anything." At this point, the truth would do more harm than good.

"Scott Sylvester Archer, you've got a choice to make."

"Shit, she's using middle names," Garrett hissed at him.

"Damn right I am, Garrett Felix Michaels. Answers. Now."

"I'll make it easy for you," Garrett said to him. "I told you I was going undercover and left a vid-message for Mena with you. You knew I didn't really resign my commission."

"True."

"You son of a..." Phyl's voice was hard, but he also recognized the jagged note in it. She was hurting too.

"You never came back, Phyl. You left on that last run and that was the last I heard from you. I sent you messages. They all bounced back. You locked me out of your comms. I even left a damned note at your favorite bar. You. Never. Came. Back."

"I had nothing to come back to. Scott, you'd made your choice when you sent Tim on that raid, even after I told you it was a trap. Garrett left the day of the funeral. I thought he'd made his choice, too."

"I was coming back."

"So, what? I was just supposed to wait for you? I lost a friend and the two men who should have been there to help me grieve for him, my lovers and his best friends, were at each other's throats."

"I had to follow orders, Phyl. You know that," Scott said. He'd lived with the consequences of that decision every hour since. In a matter of days he'd lost Tim, then Garrett, and then Phyl.

"Your orders were shit and you knew it. I had intel and you dismissed it because it came from what you deemed a questionable source."

"Are we really going to have this conversation again? While I'm on the floor, no less? Let's be civilized about this. Shall we?" Scott said and tried to push himself up. It was no good. She'd left the gravity settings too high for that.

"I'm a smuggler, Scott. I don't do civilized. While we're having this little moment of truth and consequences, did you ever tell Garrett about Tim's baby girl?"

Well. *Fraxx.* He thought he'd avoided that particular landmine. "I haven't spoken to him since he left."

Garrett gaped. "What baby? Tim had a kid? When?"

"Her name is Phaedra," Phyl said, her voice softer now.

"You knew?" Scott asked.

"You think I didn't? She's just as headstrong and smart as her daddy, and pink hair or not, the resemblance is there. Are you really so arrogant you thought no one would figure it out, or did you just think I was too dumb to notice?"

He opened his mouth, closed it, and then opened it again. No answer to that question was going to get him up off this floor. "Mostly the first one," he finally admitted. "I've been watching over that little hellion her whole life. At least, as much as her mother would let me."

"Tim has a daughter? With who? The only female he was spending time with was that waitress on Plaisa IV. Is that her mother? Tim had a little girl, and neither of you said a damned word? Starsfury. How is it I'm the one who spent years undercover and the two of you are the ones keeping all the secrets?"

"I didn't find out until later. By then, both of you were gone. I made sure she got surviving spouse benefits and set up an education fund for Phaedra." Scott glared up at Phyl. "She has no idea any of us knew Tim."

"I figured that, given she hasn't tried to kill you for depriving her of a father before she was even born."

"We all had our orders. I followed mine. Tim followed his."

Phyl sighed. "And this is why we are never going to work out. After all these years, you still haven't figured out that some orders shouldn't be followed."

"I don't get to pick and choose, Phyl. That's not how the military works."

"Still?" Garrett looked between them with something like horrified amusement. "All this time, and you two are still having that same argument? Can you at least let me up now, Mena? We've established that I did, in fact, leave a message for you and wasn't working for the evil corporations."

"You might not have been then, but you do now. I may not have your money, Garrett, or your power and influence, Scotty, but I did manage to hold on to one thing."

She pivoted on her heel and stalked toward the door. "I still have my soul."

"Phyl, you can't leave us here."

"Actually, I can. Good night, boys."

He didn't bother calling out again. He knew it wouldn't help. When Phyl got this riled, there was no talking to her. Once the door slid shut and he knew they were alone, he grunted and tried to get off the floor again. He wasn't strong enough.

Garrett tried and failed, too. "Why is this setting even possible? Who works out with this kind of gravity? Torskis?"

"And cyborgs. You should see them weightlifting in high-G. It's... impressive."

"Remind me not to piss any of them off."

"Bit late for that. You just upset their damned den mother."

"Den mother? She told me she was their mother-in-law." Garrett wasn't enjoying his current position, but he got why Phyl had done this to them. She'd taken away their ability to hit each other, so now it was talk or sulk in silence.

Fraxx. He'd missed her.

"It's an honorary term. You remember a cocky bastard named Watson? He was one of the smugglers we were chasing around the sector back then."

"Yeah. I remember. What does that have to do with anything?"

"Our spitfire hooked up with him after us. Helped raise his little girl. Zura Watson. Now Zura Armas. And her half-brother is one of Tianna Astor's trio."

"So, she's not married?"

"I just told you that Phyl hooked up with a notorious smuggler and helped raised someone else's kid, and your takeaway is she's single?"

"I was always the optimist in our relationship."

Scott managed to flop onto his back and fell back to the floor with a strained grunt. "That's one way to put it. And no, she's not single. She's seeing someone."

"Please tell me it's not that Watson guy. This reunion is crowded enough already."

"Me. She's seeing me."

"In your dreams, maybe. Or did you miss the bit where she said that the two of you would never work out."

"It's a work in progress."

"I stand corrected. If you believe that, you've become the optimist since we last met. Either that, or you're delusional." But if the only threat on the board was Scott, that meant Mena was fair game.

"Speaking of delusions, you've got a few of your own if you think Phyl is going to spend time with someone who makes their money protecting the same corporations she and her people are fighting against. Who's paying the bills this time? I know it's not Astek. Tianna would have told me if she'd hired a security consultant."

Garrett noted the name drop and decided to ignore it. "I'm on Bellex's payroll right now."

"Bellex? You're working for the assholes who micro-chipped their own workforce with explosives and drugged an entire planet to try and improve productivity? I thought you had some standards."

"They're under new management. And I am not being paid to protect the whole corporation. My job is to make sure everyone they send to this shindig comes back alive. Unlike the last time they were here." When a cyborg assassin had killed a half-dozen targets on Astek station right under Scott's nose.

"The IAF is a military organization, not a security force. We're not set up to deal with *fraxxing* assassins." Scott went quiet for a moment. "Phaedra was one of the targets. If things had gone differently that day..."

"Do you regret it?"

"Putting Phaedra at risk? Hell, yes."

"I meant Tim."

"Oh." Scott sighed, and there was a heaviness to it

Garrett had never heard before. "I miss that lunatic every damned day."

"But do you regret what happened?" It was the first time Garrett had pushed. Hell, it was the first time they'd been in the same room since the funeral.

"No. I followed orders. That's the job, Garrett. I don't get the luxury of deciding what orders to follow and which ones to ignore."

"And that's why I never came back. I *like* having that choice." It was true enough, even if it wasn't the whole truth. There'd been enough revelations today. Garrett would wait before sharing more of his.

"So, you're here until after the gala?"

"That's when my contract ends."

"Then you're leaving?" Scott didn't even try to make it sound like a casual inquiry.

"Maybe. Another of the vast benefits to being a freelancer is that I can work anywhere. If I have a reason to stay, I could stick around for a few months." Or years. At this point, he only worked to stave off boredom. He'd long since accomplished his financial goals. If he didn't work another day in his life, he'd still die a rich man.

"You're going to make a play for Phyl." It wasn't a question.

"I left her once. I'm not stupid enough to do that twice in one lifetime."

"The odds are not in your favor," Scott said.

"Since when has that stopped me? Not to mention,

she left us both trapped here. Your odds are no worse than mine, mister work-in-progress."

Scott snorted. "We always did work better as a team."

That got Garrett's full attention. "Are you suggesting..."

"Maybe. Or maybe prolonged exposure to high gravity is making my head fuzzy." Scott took an audible breath and then shouted as best he could. "Kit! I know you're there. I would appreciate it if you got your ass in here and released us now."

The door opened instantly. "She said to wait until you asked for help."

"Yeah, I figured," Scott said.

"She left the lights on," Garrett agreed. "She's not one to waste power. If we were going to be here for hours, she'd have shut them off on the way out."

"Do I want to know why she did this to you?" Kit asked.

A few seconds later the pressure vanished and Garrett took a gratifyingly deep breath.

"Difference of opinion." Scott got to his feet, shaking out his arms and legs as he rose.

"Yeah. She thought we needed a timeout. We didn't." Garrett stood, rolled his shoulders and rocked his head back and forth until his spine cracked. Between the fight and his time on the floor, he was going to need a mild pain blocker by morning. Age might bring wisdom, but he didn't enjoy other elements of it. He really needed to start inquiring about medi-bot treatments. Surely one of his clients had access to that kind of tech.

"I've been informed you two might need a drink. Bar's open. And before you ask, no, she's not waiting for you. She's gone with Zura to put the twins to bed."

"Good." Garrett massaged his jaw where Scott had landed a punch. "I'm not ready for round two yet."

"Me either." Scott looked at him. "Truce?"

"Truce. We're going to need a plan if we want to win her back."

Kit looked at them in dawning amusement. "So that's what's going on? The two of you... and Phyl? You're going to need more than a plan." The big cyborg grinned at them. "Lucky for you, you've come to the right bar. We've done this so often we've got a handbook."

"Seriously? You wrote a book on dating?" Scott asked.

"*Fraxx* no. Dating is easy. Our stuff is all about how to fix things when they blow up. Based on how I found the two of you? You're going to need all the help you can get."

"I'm not taking dating advice from a cyborg younger than my niece," Scott grumbled as they followed Kit out.

Garrett shrugged. "Why not? He's got a wife and kids. Clearly he's doing something right."

Kit snorted and then turned and held out his hand.

"I think I'm going to like you. But if you hurt Phyl, I'll still toss you out an airlock."

Garrett took the offered hand and shook it. "Message received. So, what do you know about apologizing to a woman?"

"Start with chocolate and groveling. How big an apology are you going for?"

"Thirty years' worth."

Kit whistled. "You're going to need flowers too."

"Good thing you're rich," Scott said.

"You mean it's a good thing *we're* rich."

"Yeah? In that case, there's the issue of Phylomenia's bar tab..." Kit drawled.

"She'd be able to afford to pay it off if she didn't insist on drinking that fizzy crap from Earth," Scott said with a shudder.

"She's still drinking cherry cola?" Garrett took that as a good sign. Some things hadn't changed. And as much as he wanted to go a few more rounds with Scott, he was glad to have the man back in his life. The way it had all ended had never sat right with him, and seeing how things had played out, more of that was on him than he'd realized.

He glanced over at Scott. Both the choices he had made... and the ones he hadn't been ready to make. Maybe he was going to get a chance to address both those issues in the coming days.

3

"Any chance you're going to tell me what that was about?" Zura asked in a hushed whisper as they retreated to the hallway of her quarters. The sprites were finally asleep, but they slept as lightly as their mother had when she was a child.

"Nope."

"That's fine. I'll just ask Kit."

"He doesn't know either."

"Really? Because he just let me know that your exes are at the bar, thick as thieves." Zura tapped a spot behind her ear where her new Vardarian implant sat. It let her communicate with her two cyborg husbands by an internal link, and it meant Zura was annoyingly well-informed.

"Exes? That's a nice word for those two. I prefer to

think of them as living reminders that I have terrible taste in men."

"Like my father?" Zura asked, her volume raising to near normal as they reached the main living area.

"Your father wasn't all bad."

"He did his best, but we both know who he was. No need to dip it in sugar for me."

Russ Watson had been a charming scoundrel with a weakness for women and gambling, but very little luck with either. "He loved you, though," Phyl said.

"Yes, he did. Now stop changing the subject. I knew there was history between you and Archer. I mean, it's obvious. But you and him and... what was his name again?"

"Nice try. I didn't tell you his name." Phyl dropped into her preferred chair and stretched out her legs. She'd stormed out of the gym without picking up her boots.

"Did Kit pick up my shoes while he was releasing my two... regrets from the grav-plates?"

Zura tipped her head, the deep blue of her striped markings darkening as she pretended to think. "He might have. I don't recall. Perhaps if you shared a bit more information about what happened tonight, it might help me remember."

"Stubborn brat."

"I learned from the best."

"You did. Though the flattery you learned from your daddy."

"Is it working?" Zura asked.

"Bah. You're going to learn it all from Kit, anyway. Damned cyborg hearing. I know he heard plenty even with the soundproofing. So here you go. The answer is yes. Several eons ago, I was with Scott and Garrett. So long ago I think you were about the same age your babies are now."

"What happened?"

"Scott Archer made a mistake. Not that he'll admit that's what it was."

"And that's it? You left because he made one mistake?" Zura frowned. "That's not like you."

She laughed. "Back then, I wasn't the calm, thoughtful woman I am today. I was a tank of rocket fuel just looking for a spark. Believe it or not, time has taught me tolerance and patience."

Zura blinked, her silver eyes widening dramatically. "In that case, my father was braver than I thought."

"Have I mentioned you're a brat?"

"You have, but that's not the current topic of conversation. You and Archer haven't hooked up since he got posted out here?"

"*Fraxx*, no. That ship left orbit a long time ago. We're friends now. He's married to his job, and I need a man in my life like I need a hole in my air tanks."

Zura didn't say anything. She just sat in silence for a long time. "Maybe that's the problem. What if you don't need a man in your life? What if you need two?"

Phyl ignored the little voice in the back of her mind that agreed with Zura. That voice had gotten her into most of the trouble she'd found in her life. It was not to be trusted.

"I don't need anything. I'm content with my life. Good job, kind friends." She reached out to touch Zura's hand. "Amazing family. This is more than I ever thought I'd have. I always expected me and the *Beacon* to start falling apart around the same time. One day, one of us would have a major malfunction and we'd just be one more ship lost in the big black."

"That was your plan? Keep flying until you died?" Zura's blue markings darkened. "That's a terrible plan. Even my dad managed better than that."

"Your dad had you and your lunatic brother to think about."

"And you have us. And my girls. And soon Cynder's little boy..." Zura clapped a hand to her mouth. "*Veth*. You didn't hear that."

"She told you she's having a boy?"

"Shhh! She doesn't know I know. Toro was so happy with the news he couldn't keep it a secret. He told Luke and Kit the moment he saw them and then swore them to secrecy."

"So of course, they told you."

"Of course. I'm their wife. We don't keep secrets from each other," Zura said, so primly it made Phyl laugh. Seeing the younger female happy and settled was the best part of her new life.

"I won't say a word. And not to worry, I already made my bet. Guess I'm out a bit of scrip. I wagered she was having a girl. Mostly because I wanted to see them face the same moment of terror as your men when they realized they'd be protecting their darling daughters from males just like them."

Zura laughed. "They're still terrified. They're already making plans to train Cynder's son as some sort of bodyguard to defend his older cousins."

"Like they'll need any help. They're *your* girls. You and I will teach them all they need to know about defending themselves."

"Yes we will. And Cynder will help. My girls will be able to balance the books, run a company, fly a ship, and kick the ass of anyone who messes with them."

"Damn right." Phyl waited a few moments before pivoting to a new subject. "Speaking of flying, you got anything on the books for the next few days? I've been out of the cockpit too long."

"You want to put some vacuum between you, Archer, and Garrett?"

"No. I want to work. I have grandbabies to spoil."

"Uh huh. How long do you need this work to be? I've got a shorter run that will get you back inside a week or a long haul that would keep you away until after the gala."

"A short run will be fine. You're going to need all hands on deck for the gala."

The invitees might have bigger parties and

meetings to attend, but everyone coming would bring their own solar system of support staff and followers. When those folks weren't working, they'd be looking for food, drink, and a place to indulge their vice of choice.

"We're hoping it's busy. It will have to be to make up for lost business. Most of the mining crews are staying clear until this is over. Did you know short-term docking prices have doubled lately? There's only so much room to dock on this station. Soon every berth is going to be taken until this party is over."

"Tianna know about that?"

"She does. She said it was done deliberately. Something about keeping the station's visitor population down for that time period."

"That's a little foreboding," Phyl said. It fit with some other things she'd seen lately, though.

"She's planning something. Isn't she?"

"The gala is more than just a party and peace talks," Phyl agreed.

"Too many targets for the Grays to ignore." Zura's gaze flitted to the door of her daughters' bedroom.

"Maybe Royan and your men were right. Now would be a good time for you and the sprites to visit Haven. I know Phaedra would love to see you." And it would get three of the beings she loved most in the world away from whatever trouble was coming.

"Nope. You know I've already done this dance

with them. This is my fight, too. My home. I'm not leaving."

"Stubborn."

"But smart. I'll make sure the *Sun Sprite* is fully stocked and ready to fly. If things get ugly, I'll head for my ship and bring my family with me. *All* of them."

"Between your ship and mine, we can house most of the Nova staff and their families."

"Good thing I own a shipping company. I'll make sure enough of my vessels are docked to act as sanctuaries for everyone we care about. Just in case."

"Let's hope we don't need them."

Zura nodded. "Hope for the best but always assume the universe is out to get you."

"You know, I'm starting to realize your daddy was a very cynical man." Phyl got to her feet. "When do I leave and where am I flying?"

"Tomorrow afternoon. It was a last-minute arrangement, so the timing is tight. You're headed to Tangar Nine. Outgoing cargo is fragile but stable. Return is frozen goods."

She grinned. "Dag's sending us another shipment of fresh steaks?"

"He is. And bacon. Real bacon. Now if we could just find a connection we could import eggs from, we'd have the best breakfasts in the quadrant."

"What did that cost you?"

"Two crates of Pheran frost wine and a whole bunch of seeds for plants I've never heard of. You have any idea what a jicama is? And something called a zoochinee."

"Zucchini," Phyl said absently.

"What the *fraxx* is a zucchini and why is it pronounced nothing like it's spelled?"

"Earth plant. Bit like a cucumber but bigger. A lot bigger. Some of the colonies still grow them. And as for why it's pronounced that way, I have no idea. Some words predate Galactic Standard."

"Score one for standardized trade languages." Zura yawned and then rose to walk Phyl to the door.

"Can you send me the inventory list and documentation I'll need first thing in the morning? If this is a tight turn-around, I might as well try and get an early start."

"Of course. We both know how much you love mornings." Zura's tone was so dry she might have been chewing on moondust.

Phyl loathed mornings. She was a night owl by nature and years of flying solo had left her with a preference for silence. Mornings, at least on a station like Astek, were chaotic, noisy, and full of beings so chipper they had to be doing pharma. "I'll make an exception if it means fresh steak when I get back."

"You know, I almost believed you. Now go. Get some sleep. Apparently you're going to be up early tomorrow morning."

It would be easier to face an early morning than it would be to deal with Scott and Garrett when they were getting along. A week away should be long enough for them to remember the lesson they'd clearly forgotten... the only reason they got along was because she'd always kept the peace between them. With her gone, they'd fall into old habits. By the time she got back, they'd have reverted to their usual form of communication... insults and fist fights.

Zura was right. She'd never had a problem dealing with one male at a time. It was when she let two of them into her heart things had gotten messy. It was a mistake she wouldn't make again.

The Nova Club's VIP section was like an oasis of calm after the barrage of music and conversation that filled the rest of the club. Garrett had a quick moment of gratitude for whoever had set up the sound dampeners in this area. The technology allowed just a hint of music to carry through while also ensuring that every table had privacy to talk.

Food, drink, pharma, and just about anything else that was more or less legal this far out could be ordered through the digital menu at each table or requested from one of the wait staff who wandered by every few minutes. From their table they had a view of both the docking rings outside and the fight cage set up on a lower floor.

"This is a hell of a setup. I thought space was at a

premium out here," Garrett said once they were settled.

"It is." Scott inclined his head toward the cage below. "Fight nights here are big money. They've signed some of the best talent around and put on a great show. The crowds love it, and the betting is crazy. Toss in the sim-pod rentals, licensed pharma dealers, the casino, and a constant flow of hard-working miners and flight crews looking to have some fun before their next year-long mission starts? This place is a gold mine. One with a lot of overhead."

"And it's also the home of the biggest thorns in the corporations' sides."

"And that, too. But it's the most secure place on the station. The Armas crew might be crazy, but they're smart, loyal, and protect their own," Scott said.

"Is that the sound of grudging respect I hear? High praise coming from you."

"It's also the sound of me warning you to step carefully. Phyl's part of their family. If you *fraxx* with her..." he shrugged and didn't finish his sentence.

"Yeah, Kit made that clear already. But I'm not here to screw up her life. Hell, I didn't know she was here at all. You, I was prepared for. She was a surprise."

"So you knew I was here and didn't bother to send me a heads up?" Archer didn't look impressed.

Garrett didn't care. He spread his hands and shrugged. "I'm your ten o'clock appointment tomorrow.

I wanted to see your face when I walked into your office."

"I don't recall your name being mentioned."

"I'm listed as the Bellex security advisor. I didn't want to spoil the surprise." He raised his hands to his shoulders, fingers splayed, and grinned. "Surprise."

"Ass."

"And now we're on familiar ground. All that's missing is a couple of drinks. You still pretending to like brandy?" he asked.

"You still drinking cocktails that only appeal to someone with the palate of a six-year-old?" Scott shot back.

"I still like Venusian Sunrises, yes. But I think tonight calls for something a little more subtle." He scanned the list, impressed by both the caliber and extent of the bar's offerings. He made his selection, adding a few appetizers to the order before sending it to the kitchen. A quick touch of his comm unit transferred the payment information, and then his focus was back on Scott.

His friend looked good. Time had been kind to him, though his hair was almost pure silver now, and the lines around his eyes deepened when he scowled. They weren't laugh lines. Long hours and the burdens of command had etched each mark into his skin.

"Do I get to know what you just ordered or is this another *surprise*?"

"There was a time you liked it when I took charge

of things." It wasn't the smartest thing he could have said, but if they were doing this, he needed to know what exactly the stakes were going to be.

"I don't let anyone manage me these days. It's not a good look for a colonel."

"You're more than your rank, Scott. All these years and you still haven't figured that out?"

"The only people who believed that both left." Scott shrugged. "So I went with what I knew."

"You're an idiot."

"Says the man who turned a short-term undercover op into a career. How long did you stay on the IAF payroll before you turned traitor and joined the corporate world for real?"

"Longer than you think." All the paperwork said he'd left the day he walked away from Scott and Phylomenia. The reality was something quite different.

"You were always looking for a way to get rich."

"And you were always trying to gather more power. Looks like we both got what we thought we wanted."

A server came by with their drink order, setting down two glasses and a bottle of fifteen-year-old whiskey first before adding two shot glasses of dark red liquor.

"Is that what I think it is?" Archer asked, a smile ghosting over his lips.

"Torski Star Blood." He raised his shot glass in a toast. "To unexpected reunions and new possibilities."

"New possibilities... including the possibility I'm going to need to order a new liver after I drink this."

"Drink it, you wuss." Garrett tossed his back and tried not to wince as the shot burned a path down his throat before erupting with volcanic heat as it mixed with his stomach acid.

Scott did the same, both of them keeping their expressions carefully neutral as long as they could.

It wasn't until Garrett's eyes started to water that he gave up the attempt and burst out laughing. "Damn it. I was sure I'd win this time."

"Never going to happen." Scott set his empty shot glass on the table. "Though I don't recall it being that damned uncomfortable the last time we did this."

"We were younger and dumber back then." Garrett waited in silence as the server returned to retrieve their empty glasses and set out several plates of food. Both of them went straight for the bread, eating several bites to calm their stomachs before anything else was said.

"I take it you don't have medi-bots, then? It feels strange to think that Phyl actually adopted a technology before either of us."

"Not yet. You know how long it takes for the IAF to decide to embrace anything new. By the time they finish testing, re-testing, forming several committees and debating it all, I'll be long retired."

"Then where'd she get hers?"

"The Armas crew included one of the original

designers of the medi-bots. He saw to it they all had access. Forced everyone's hand. The corporations killed him for it."

"Ah. Right. Zale." He'd read all the reports and now he was putting together the facts he knew with the reality of this place and these beings.

"Zale. Ironic, really. The Vardarians use similar tech. Once they arrived, there was never any chance of keeping the nanotech away from the general population. It's just a matter of time now."

"Before every corporation will have a work force that can work harder, faster, and live for hundreds of years?" That's what his clients were all hoping for. He hoped for something better... for everyone.

"That's one way it could unfold." Scott paused to take a drink of his whiskey before saying anything more.

"You don't think that's what's going to happen?" Garrett asked.

"I think in a few generations we're going to have an entire galaxy of beings who live for hundreds of years no matter what species they are. That means resources and infrastructure are going to be taxed to the breaking point. Exploration will be a matter of necessity. New colonies will arise. New wars will break out over territory and trade. It's going to get ugly."

"And the corporations? What do you think they'll do?"

"I don't know. I was hoping you might have some

insight. I know what Tianna Astor wants to happen. She's hosting this whole damned party to try and get everyone to agree to set aside their differences and find a new way forward."

"They'll agree to anything, so long as it doesn't interfere with their profit margins."

"That's what I'm afraid of. They've managed to create a system that can keep their workforce indebted to them for most of a lifetime. Sometimes even for generations. But how is that going to work when everyone lives for centuries?"

"You think there will be a breaking point." Garrett had the same thought. Though no one had said anything to him, he would bet good scrip that's why so many of the corporations had agreed to attend the upcoming gala. As much as they liked the idea of an immortal workforce, the smart ones were worried that wasn't going to be how it played out.

"Breaking point might be too gentle a word. There's likely to be an uprising. And you know what happens during those," Scott said.

"A lot of innocent people die."

"And governments tend to get overthrown."

"That's your department," Garrett said, downing a drink.

"Protecting corporate lackeys is yours. Do you think the government will be the only one targeted if things go that far?"

Garrett lowered his voice. "I don't. Which is why

I've been considering retirement. Protecting my clients from each other is one thing, but I don't want to be the one they're hiding behind when an angry mob comes looking for vengeance."

He hadn't said the words aloud to anyone else until now. The thought was made much more real the moment it left his mouth. It was time for a change. Find something else to do that didn't involve assessing every room he walked into for threats and knowing every friend he'd ever had believed he'd sold his soul to the corporations. Even his own family thought that's what he'd done. Oh, they'd accepted his gifts and settled onto the farm he'd bought, but he saw it in their eyes. The sadness and disappointment were easy to spot.

"That... might be the smartest thing I've ever heard you say," Scott said.

"What about you? Retirement some day? Or are you planning to die at your desk, still wearing the uniform?"

Scott's mask dropped, and for a moment Garrett saw him clearly. Tired, proud, and more than a little lost. "This is all I'm good at. If I retire, I'd be bored in a week and dead in a month."

Without thinking, he reached out and gripped Scott's hand. "That's not all you're good at."

For one brief, perfect moment, Scott squeezed his hand back, but then he withdrew from Garrett's touch.

It was enough to give him hope—stupid, reckless,

idiotic hope. He carried on as if nothing had happened. "Besides, if you manage to win our spitfire back, you'd never be bored. We always said it would take two of us to keep that one out of trouble, and you were going to try and manage her on your own."

"I hoped." Scott shrugged. "But now you're here." He took another drink. "You're really thinking about retiring?"

"I am."

"Then this might actually work. The three of us, I mean."

"So, we're doing this?"

"We're going to try. The lady in question did leave us pinned to a floor not long ago."

"The lady in question is no lady. She's our spitfire. Always has been."

Scott nodded and raised his glass. "Always will be."

Now all they had to do was convince Phylomenia of that. "Do you think Kit was kidding about that book of dating advice?"

Scott shook his head. "I have no idea. Let's ask him and find out."

4

Scott hadn't slept well. It had been impossible to rest when every time he closed his eyes he heard Phyl say they would have never worked out. The few times he'd actually managed to doze off, he'd dreamed of Garrett reaching for his hand over and over.

He'd given up and gone back to work. Not even the stack of work he had to do could stop him from thinking about last night for more than a few minutes. Frustrated, he rose from his desk and paced several circuits around his office. "I am too old for this shit. Love is a young man's game."

He looked back at the files displayed over his desk. He had the usual reports and paperwork, but among the digital clutter was a missive confirming that the first doses of military medi-bots were almost ready. He'd lied to Garrett about that. He'd had to. Their creation was a carefully guarded secret. The research and development had all taken place here on Astek instead of the IAF's labs. Hiding in plain sight seemed like the best idea, and it allowed the researchers direct access to two doctors with extensive experience dealing with the medi-bots: Dr. Alyson Jeffries and Dr. Tyra Li. Alyson was married to a trio of cyborgs, and Tyra was living with Dante Strak, one of the members of the Nova Force team stationed on Astek.

Soon, he'd need to decide. One of those doses was earmarked for him if he wanted it. It would mean extending his service to the IAF, but that wasn't a problem. Like he'd told Garrett last night, he didn't have anything else but the job.

The issue was more basic than that. If he took the dose, there was a good chance he'd outlive most of the beings he knew. This technology wouldn't be commonplace for years. Possibly decades.

Phyl had the nanotech already, though. He wouldn't be entirely alone. They could be together... All three of them. Somehow. Maybe.

Fraxx.

He swiped a hand through the display, making the images flicker. He'd only been in one trio in his life, and that one hadn't been planned. Since then, he kept his affairs brief, uncomplicated, and discreet.

Getting tangled up with Phyl again would be none of those things. He'd known that when he'd decided to try and win her back. He'd thought it was going well, if slowly. As was usually the case when it came to Phylomenia, he'd been wrong.

Maybe it would be smarter to step back and let Garrett try on his own.

No. He rejected the idea before it was fully formed. No way in hell was he letting Garrett take Phyl away from him.

He snorted in derision as he recognized that history was repeating itself. This was how the three of them had ended up together in the first place. Neither of them would let Phyl go, so they'd agreed to a trio. It had led to the best months of his life and the realization that his friendship with Garrett was evolving into something more.

Then it had all gone wrong.

Tim's death was a burden he'd carried every day since, but regret wouldn't bring his friend back. Orders were orders. He chose to trust the IAF's intel because once he questioned one order, it would be too easy to question others.

The rules for advancing in the military were uncannily similar to the ones for getting on with his family. One had to appear confident at all times and not do anything that could be perceived as disloyalty. Be exceptional but conform to expectations. He'd seen what happened when someone broke ranks. In the IAF, it meant a lifetime of postings to the most isolated, unpleasant spots in the galaxy. With his family, it was even worse. His older sister was never mentioned. Her name had been struck from the family history as if she'd never existed. All because she'd wanted to choose her own path and go to law school.

Thoughts of his sister brought him back to another task he needed to address today.

"Computer, locate Lieutenant Commander Castille and inform her I need a word with her. In person. My office. Coordinate schedules, but make it sometime today."

"Order confirmed."

He might not be able to offer the medi-bot treatment to many, but he could pull a few strings and make sure his favorite niece had the option. She'd placed herself in a risky position for him, and this was one of the few ways he could try to protect her while still keeping their relationship, and the fact she was working for him, a secret.

These days he was keeping so many secrets it felt like the truth had become a liquid instead of solid. It shifted and flowed depending on who he spoke with and what they already knew. He'd brought his niece Bobbi into the equation because he needed someone he could trust, someone from outside who might see things differently.

His plans with Tianna Astor were another set of secrets. They'd worked together to set up this gala, creating a target too tempting for their adversaries to resist. They still had things they couldn't be entirely open about, but she'd agreed to let Nova Force operatives on the premises to track the entire event. In return, he'd agreed to allow her own security to work with IAF personnel to make sure that no matter what happened, the risk would be minimized.

He was ordering up a fresh mug of coffee from his food dispenser when the computer chimed softly. "Colonel Archer, your ten o'clock appointment has arrived twenty-nine minutes early." The AI wasn't capable of being annoyed, but a buzz in the synthesized voice hinted the program wasn't pleased with the unexpected interruption.

"Clear my desktop display and then send him in." Scott punched a second order into the dispenser, his fingers moving faster than his brain. Dark roast. Double sweet. Heavy cream. He had no idea if Garrett drank his coffee that way anymore. In fact, he barely knew the man. It was yet another reason he should not even be considering what they were about to do.

Garrett strode through the door the moment it opened. His suit was perfectly tailored, flattering every inch of his still-damned-attractive body. Broad shoulders, trim waist. Nice... *no.* He wasn't going there. Not yet, anyway.

"I know what you're going to say, so let me summarize for you. Yes, I am early. Stars, yes, I need a coffee. Thanks for offering." Garrett spoke as if they were already in the middle of a conversation.

Scott handed the mug to him. "Your suit is... purple. Seriously. Who dresses you?"

"Bless you." Garrett took a sip and groaned. "A double-double. You remembered. And the suit is black with subtle tones of violet and dove gray, thank you. I'm dressed by the best."

"It's purple. And how could I forget the sacrilege that is your preferred way to drink coffee?"

"I suppose you still drink yours dark as the void outside and entirely lacking anything interesting?"

"Actually, I like it with sweetener these days."

"You changed? Miracles abound."

"Don't be an asshole. You're in my office, drinking my coffee. Behave."

"And there's the bossy senior officer I remember." Garrett dropped his big bulk into a nearby chair with surprising grace and raised his mug. "So, have you gotten to the part where you've decided this is a terrible idea and you're not going to do it?"

"I'm past that. I've now decided it's an insane idea that is doomed to fail, but why the hell not? Plus, I intend to blame you when this blows up in our faces."

"Yet, as I recall, this was your idea."

Scott sat down at his desk. "Nope. I'm certain this was all on you. Of course, that recollection could change if this actually works."

"Of course it will. This idea of... mine. What was the plan again? I'm a little fuzzy on the details."

Scott snorted. "That's because we drank a bottle of

very fine whiskey and another round of Star Blood. Also because we didn't come up with a plan. We ended up reminiscing instead."

"And catching up. Lots of that. Mostly you because your life has been rather dull and you covered the highlights in less than ten minutes."

"It was at least half an hour, asshole. Drink your coffee," Scott grumbled.

"Gladly. So, plan? We need one."

"We're dating her, not planning an invasion. It doesn't need to be complicated. We ask her out for dinner. Make sure it's somewhere without sharp utensils, heavy objects, or grav-plates with easily accessible controls."

"Are you sure this isn't an invasion?" Garrett asked, chuckling. "Recommendations on where to take her?" His tone bordered on command.

Scott bristled. "You do remember that I outrank you?" Scott tapped the insignia on his uniform.

"I'm a tax-paying citizen, which means that technically, I pay your salary. I think that makes me your boss. So, I'm asking my underling what restaurants he recommends."

"You call me your underling again and we're going back to the Nova Club so I can finish giving you the beat down I started handing out last night."

"Please. Phyl was saving you from me, not the other way around. And if we're doing this, we need a better plan than just taking her out to dinner. For starters, if things go well, whose place are we going back to? My hotel has a large bed, clean sheets, and room service. Unless the IAF has seriously improved their standards, I'm betting you've got a smallish bed in a smallish room with prefab furniture that's probably all blue."

"Some of it's gray. And since I'm the highest-ranking officer in the sector, I have three rooms."

"I have a suite. Also, no security check points to pass through."

"That is a good point. About the security, I mean. Discretion is important." He didn't want the people under his command thinking he was distracted by a romance when the entire station was on high alert. Not to mention the fact that Garrett was a security risk. This was going to be complicated.

Some things hadn't changed.

Garrett watched Scott's expression and could almost read the thoughts as they spooled through his head. The man was still a mess of conflicting needs, wanting things he didn't believe he could have.

Garrett had left because he thought his friend chose duty over friendship and love. Now, with the clarity of age and hindsight, he saw something different. Ambition didn't drive Scott Archer but the belief he didn't deserve anything else. That's why he hadn't really tried to win back Phylomenia. Why he was still alone after all this time.

Or maybe he's been waiting for us...

Garrett dragged his mind back to the conversation at hand. "Then if all the stars align, we'll take her back to my place."

"Big if."

"So now we figure out how to improve the odds. At least this time, we're working together from the start. Imagine how much better things would have gone if we hadn't been competing against each other last time?"

"Not all of us were raised in poly families. Sharing honestly never occurred to me until you suggested it. Speaking of which, I always wondered. Given you had two fathers, why did it take you so long to float the idea of a trio?"

"Because some ambitious and very proper young officer I knew had drilled it into my head that to get ahead, one had to fit in."

Scott wrinkled his nose. "So, that's on me, too?"

"Not entirely. We all made mistakes."

Scott went silent. "I thought it was the right call."

"Which part? Ignoring Phyl's intel or the fact that you both kept me out of the loop completely? He was my friend, too."

"That's not what—"

Garrett didn't let him finish. "Don't. Just. Don't. She came to you in secret. You made your decision without telling me what Phyl knew. The first I heard of it was when the two of you were fighting like a pair of rabid dogs. It was a shitty way to find out that you were both keeping secrets from me."

"You realize that isn't going to change. Right? We're not even on the same side anymore. There are going to be things we can't talk about."

"Was that an apology? It didn't sound like one."

"I didn't know she hadn't told you. Honestly, I figured you two were working together. You always did have more in common with her than I did."

Garrett managed to inhale his coffee instead of swallowing it and burst into a fit of coughing. Once his lungs were clear again, he replied, "Me? You two were both pilots. You had *everything* in common."

They stared at each other for several long seconds, and then Scott started to laugh. "So, we were both idiots."

"Apparently. Damn. I've missed you."

Scott rose and held out his hand. Garrett took it, surprised when his friend pulled him to his feet and clapped him into a firm hug. "This time, we'll do it better."

"We have to. I don't know if the universe is going to give us a third chance to get this right." He didn't just mean Phylomenia, either. Not this time. If they were doing this again, he was going to be greedy. He wanted them both.

Half an hour later they were walking into the Nova Club armed with flowers, determination, and a decent plan.

It wasn't even noon yet, but the place was almost as busy as it had been last night. Astek station, and the rest of the Drift, officially operated on a twenty-four-hour day, but the reality was that day and night meant nothing in a place with no sun to rise or set. Time was entirely relative out here, so most shops stayed at least partially open at all times. That oddity of station life always took some getting used to.

A blond man with a military bearing and a stormy scowl stepped into Scott's path before they were more than halfway across the room. "If those are for Chance, she's still in bed after the last session you put her through. Flowers aren't going to help her recover."

"Relax, O'Neill. I'm not here for her. I know that last one was difficult, and I'm sorry she's still recovering. I've already given orders to reduce her exposure per session to half what she took on last time. It was too much. The tech who opened the files to her has been moved to another project."

"Oh. Good." The scowl lightened. "Uh. Thanks."

"Please tell me this is a work thing," Garrett said, trying to work out what he was going to do if it wasn't.

"What? Oh, yes. Chance is a consultant. Let's try this again, shall we? Erik O'Neill, this is Garrett Michaels. He's freelance corporate security. We're here to see Phyl, actually. Have you seen her?"

Erik shook his head. "Sorry to be the bearer of bad news. Phyl's gone."

"*Gone?* Gone where? The *Beacon* wasn't due for another run until after the gala." Scott's tone echoed the sinking feeling in Garrett's chest. Their spitfire had bolted on them. Again.

"I'm just club security. I know she's gone because I was on shift when she left. Other than that? I have no information. You need to talk to Zura."

Scott just nodded. "Make it happen."

Erik raised one brow. "Magic word?"

"Please," Scott said with an exasperated sigh. "Could you please let Zura know we'd like to talk to her?"

"Of course. Take a seat in the VIP section while you wait."

"Thank you."

"Appreciate it," Garrett added.

They grabbed the same table they'd had the night before. It looked smaller now with the flowers taking up most of the space.

"She did it again," Garrett grumbled.

"She did. But maybe that's not such a bad thing. After all, this time we know she'll be back. Her family is here. This just gives us time to come up with a proper plan."

Garrett nodded to the flowers. "We had a plan."

"We did, but I'm starting to think you were right after all."

"Miracles abound yet again," Garrett joked.

"Ass. I meant about the plan. This isn't just dinner anymore. This is a full military engagement with a dangerous and elusive adversary."

"So, we *are* invading?"

"We are," Scott said.

"Us and what army?"

"This one." Scott gestured around them. "Because if I know one thing about the Nova Club crew, it's this. They will do anything for family."

Now this sounded promising. "So, we're going to ask them to help us win over Phylomenia?"

"If you agree."

"Oh, I agree. I'm just astounded this was your idea."

"Some things haven't changed, my friend." Scott grinned at him, suddenly looking decades younger. "Some things have."

Garrett ignored the flutter in his stomach as he watched Scott. "Do you think they'll actually help?"

"Let's ask and find out." Scott pointed to a small, blue-skinned female headed their way. "And a word to the wise. This one might not be Phyl's kin by blood, but they're kin in every way that matters, including temperament."

"Noted. Do you think she likes flowers?" he nodded to the forlorn bouquet on the table.

"Let's hope so." Scott turned toward the new

arrival and smiled with uncustomary warmth. "Morning, Zura."

"Archer. Mr. Michaels. I believe you were looking for Phyl?" Her gaze dropped to the flowers and she winced slightly. "I wondered if she'd told you. I guess not."

"If you like the flowers, take them. She won't be back before they're wilted. Will she?"

"Afraid not. That run takes about a week."

"Her idea?" Garrett asked, already knowing the answer.

"Of course. She shouldn't have left until this afternoon, but she insisted on an early start." Zura grinned. "You two must be something else. I've never seen Phyl run from a fight before."

"We have," Scott said, a note of regret in his voice.

"But this time, we're not giving up so easily." Garrett picked up the flowers and handed them to Zura. "Care to join the campaign? We could use your help."

The pretty little female beamed at them, the gleam in her silver eyes reminding him of Phylomenia just before she announced a new plan. "I thought you'd never ask."

5

GETTING AWAY FROM THE STATION HAD SEEMED like a good idea—an easy run to a friendly destination and plenty of time to let Scott and Garrett remember all the reasons why they drove each other crazy. It was a solid plan, or so she thought.

Phylomenia had spent most of the trip pacing the decks of her ship, wondering what was happening back on Astek.

The gala was only a week away. The station would be full of beings from all over the galaxy. Was the club handling the influx alright? Were the corporations at each other's throats yet? With everything going on, was Zura getting enough time with the twins? Was Cynder resting like she was supposed to? Cynder was going to be the first cyborg to give birth. She should be fine, but no one knew for sure because it had never happened before.

Zura wasn't any help, either. Every time Phylomenia checked in she got a brief hello, a distracted update on some minor issue, and then the call would end with Zura claiming one of the sprites was fussy and needed her.

Either the twins had suddenly turned into tiny tyrants, or Zura was deliberately avoiding her.

"I need to get home," she declared to the empty air, as if expressing her wish aloud could somehow change the laws of physics. She was on final approach to the Drift now, and that meant standard engines only. Activating jump-engines this close to so much traffic was a recipe for disaster, and anyone who tried it and survived was met with stiff fines and the risk of being banned from local space.

She drummed her fingers against the console in front of her, eyes on the viewscreen where Astek Station was barely more than a blip. Still an hour out, she estimated and then checked the readouts to confirm. One hour and three minutes until she reached port.

"Screw it, close enough." She was about to request a vid-connection to Zura when an incoming message arrived. Phyl checked the caller ID and grinned. It was Zura.

"I was just about to let you know I'm on final approach. Should be there in about an hour."

"I figured you were due soon and had a free moment, so I thought I'd check in. I've arranged for the *Beacon* to be docked next to the *Sun Sprite*. Once we have your cargo off-loaded, I'll get both ships restocked like we talked about before you left. The rest of the ships are either already prepped or on longer runs that should keep them clear until after the gala ends."

"You still expecting trouble?"

Zura wrinkled her nose. It was a small expression, but one Phylomenia knew well. "There's a new problem. It's not affecting us directly, but you should probably be aware."

"What? What's going on? Everything okay at the club?" She couldn't shake the feeling something was going to happen soon. It was why she wanted to get back home. She needed to be there if, or more likely when, things went wrong.

"We're all fine. Busy as *fraxx,* but that's to be expected. Astek's party might not have officially started, but the station is already packed with new arrivals. Between the new guests and the military, tensions are running high."

"I'm not surprised. Does Archer know?"

"I assume so, but it's not like I'm going to tell him how to do his job. I don't know him well enough for that." She gave Phylomenia a pointed look. "Unlike some people I could name."

"Well played. I didn't even see the hook in that bait

until I'd already swallowed it. Alright, I'll talk to him. I make no promises he'll listen, but I'll try."

"Thanks." Zura smiled. "Oh, and you might want to shower and change on board. The demand for water on the station is higher than ever. These VIPs have no idea what conservation means."

"Noted. Remind me to stay in the club for the next week. I have no interest in rubbing elbows or any other body parts with the high and mighty of the galaxy."

"Not even a certain security expert you know?"

"Definitely not him. Please tell me he hasn't been sniffing around the club trying to find out where I am or when I'll be back?"

"He came around the day you left. We took care of things. It's all good."

Phyl wasn't sure if she was happy or disappointed by that news. "I'm glad you took care of it. This ship does not fly in any direction but forward, and that means no trips back to the good old days."

"Very sensible. Not in the slightest bit romantic, though." Zura winked. "He *is* hot. And Archer isn't bad either."

"You did not just say that!" Someone, Phylomenia thought it was Luke, bellowed from out of view.

"Oh, she did. And now she's going to pay for it." Kit popped into the frame and lifted his wife out of her chair. "Bye, Phyl. Zura will not be meeting you when you dock. We'll send Cyn to do the paperwork."

"Yeah, Cyn. Zura will be busy. Very, very busy," Luke agreed.

Zura laughed and waved. "Oops. I forgot about cyborg hearing. Bye, Phyl!"

Phylomenia ended the call and chuckled. "Like hell you forgot."

Still, it was good to see Zura so happy. That one had picked well. Good men. They were devoted to her and their babies and almost never let their egos get the better of their common sense, unlike some males she knew.

With nothing to do until the final docking sequence, Phyl left the ship on autopilot and went to grab a long, hot shower. Maybe she could scrub all her wayward thoughts of Scott and Garrett out of her head before she got back to the station.

Maybe.

Docking went so smoothly she could have let the AI handle the chore, but that would have left her with nothing to do for the last fifteen minutes. She was almost looking forward to the noise and bustle of the club. Normally she preferred things quieter, but she'd had enough peace and quiet for now. She needed distractions. Lots of them. The louder, the better.

Bag over her shoulder, she made her way to the cargo bay to meet Cynder. New station rules stated that all shipments had to be signed for by a representative from the shipping company or the receiver, and it had to be someone other than the pilot.

It also had to be done in person, and only after everything had been inspected and verified.

The theory was it would cut down on smuggling. It might have worked, too, except any smuggler with experience already hid their contraband or made sure that the ones signing were paid to look the other way.

A touch of her hand activated the cargo bay doors. They grumbled like an old man rising from his chair before opening. She'd need to get them looked at and repaired. The whole ship would need to be overhauled soon. It was already well past its life expectancy, but she wasn't ready to let the old girl go. They'd been through too much together.

Cynder was through the doors before they'd reached the halfway mark. "Hey. Good trip?"

"Smooth as *keski* silk. I even managed to snag a nice steak dinner before heading out again."

"Great. Just a few things I need to go over before I can sign off on this cargo." Cynder's grin turned wicked.

"Come in, guys."

"You wouldn't..." Phyl trailed off as Scott and Garrett stepped through the doors together, both of them grinning like lunatics. "*Fraxxing* hell. You would. You did." She pointed a finger at Cynder. "You and Zura are *helping* them? You're my family. I trusted you."

"We are. We love you, and we want to see you happy. So..." Cynder held up a data tablet. "Once we go through this checklist, I'll sign off on the cargo and you're free to leave. With them."

"Blackmail? Really?" She turned her attention to the men. "You're willing to stoop this low?"

"As low as it takes," Garrett said.

"You left. *Again*," Scott said. "So in order to prevent the past from repeating itself, we called in some expert help."

"Tricksters and traitors. All of you." She folded her arms across her chest and leaned against the back wall as casually as she could. There wasn't a snowball's chance in hell she was going to let them see how off balance she was right now. They were here. For her. Her stubborn and oh so proud pair of exes were not only getting along with each other, they'd somehow managed to swallow their pride and enlist the help of her family.

It was almost as flattering as it was disconcerting.

"Checklist time. Is all the cargo present and accounted for?" Cynder asked.

"It is. You can check the ship's manifest if you like."

"No need. I trust you." Cyn's tone was all business, but there was no missing the grin flirting around the corners of her mouth. She was enjoying this.

"That brings us to the next item. Archer, you're up."

Scott stepped forward and offered her a garment bag that he'd held draped over one arm. "For tonight. If you would do us the honor of wearing this dress?"

She took the bag without comment and tried to hide her surprise when she realized that Scott had forgone his uniform and even his preferred color scheme. He wore gray slacks and a charcoal gray sweater of some soft fabric that clung to his fit body in ways any woman could appreciate.

A quick check revealed that the bag contained one of her favorite outfits, and one of the few dresses she owned. "How did you get this?"

"Zura and I picked the dress. It's the same one you wore to both our weddings and you look amazing in it," Cynder said.

"So long as neither of them were poking through my closet. Alright. I'm accepting the dress. Do I get to know where I'm wearing it?"

"Not yet. Patience, spitfire. We'll get there." Garrett's tone held a hint of command that made her heart flutter.

Veth, she used to love it when he'd used that tone on her... or on Scott.

"And that's your cue, Michaels," Cynder prompted.

Scott stepped back and Garrett moved into his spot. He wore dark pants, knee-high boots, and a crisp white shirt with subtle pinstripes of blue and green that matched his eyes—one green, one blue, both sparkling with enjoyment.

He held out a cream-colored piece of paper—actual paper—that had been folded in half. "For you. An

invitation to join us for an evening of dating delights."
He winked at her. "Starting with dinner and ending...
well... that is up to you, Mena."

She ignored the way her cheeks heated and
dropped her head to read the invitation. It was
handwritten, a rarity in and of itself. It invited her, in
the most formal language she'd seen outside of a legal
contract, to accompany Scott and Garrett to dinner,
dancing, and enjoyment. At least, that was the gist of it.
When she read the location, she swore softly. Amped.
"So, they're in on it too?"

Garrett managed to look both confused and
innocent at the same time, which was a hell of a trick
when she knew he was neither. "Who's in on what?"

"Amped. That place has a waiting list even on
quiet nights, and there's no way this station is quiet
right now."

"I called in a favor," Scott said. "I do know plenty
of beings on this station."

"Most of whom I introduced you to," she replied
dryly. "How deep does this conspiracy go?"

"Get dressed and you can find out for yourself,"
Cynder said.

"You're really going to hold my cargo hostage until
I go through with this?"

"That's the plan." Cynder's smile faded. "Unless
you really don't want to do this. We'd never force you,
Phyl. So if this is not what you want, all you have to do
is say so."

Scott moved in beside Garrett and both of them held out a hand to her. "It's your call, spitfire. If this really isn't what you want, this ends now."

Fraxx. They were calling her bluff. If she said no, they'd respect her decision, which was as it should be. But she knew these two too well to miss their unspoken point. If she pushed them away tonight, that was it. No more chances to revisit the past on a whirlwind reunion tour.

She gave herself to the count of three before committing herself to the winds of chaos and second chances and took both their hands. "This might be the last chance I get to have the two of you treat me to a night out on the town—or what passes for it around here. I'm in."

"Which brings us to the end of my checklist. Gentlemen, if you would finalize this arrangement?"

Both men smiled, and Phyl suddenly knew what a mouse felt like when faced with a pair of hungry cats.

In a move so perfect they must have practiced, they raised her hands to their lips and brushed a gentle kiss to her knuckles. Then, they both drew something out of their pockets and showed it to her. Two identical bracelets made of interwoven strands of delicate metal. They were elegant yet simple, and very much her style.

"Jewelry? You could have just gone with flowers, you know."

Both men slipped a bangle onto her wrist and then

released her, stepping back and giving her room to admire her new gifts.

"We tried that. The lady in question departed before we could make delivery. It worked out, though. Zura was happy to accept them as a token of our gratitude for helping us plan this," Scott said.

"You bribed her with *my* flowers?"

"You were on an urgent mission to retrieve cold cuts," Garrett pointed out. "The flowers would have wilted before you got back."

"Speaking of cold, you better out of here and into that dress, Phyl. You have a hot date to get to and I'd like to start offloading the cargo. Once I open the lower hold, it's going to get very cold in here. You delicate humans won't enjoy it."

"I'll meet you at the main door in five minutes." It wouldn't take her long to change. She'd already showered and... son of a starbeast. Zura was too clever for her own good sometimes. "Cyn, how's the water pressure at the club?"

Cynder's smile was an answer all on its own. "Perfectly fine. Why?"

Phyl snorted with laughter. "I've just realized how neatly I've been managed. I love you both, but don't think for one moment that will save you."

"It's a risk we're willing to take. Go get dressed."

Garrett chuckled. "You should have seen them, Phyl. They ran this like a military campaign."

"Speaking of running. I think I'll hang on to your

last present a little while longer. Incentive for you to stick around this time," Scott said.

"No running. Not tonight. You have my word. But hold on to the present anyway. We really do need to get out of here. Cyn can handle subzero temperatures. I don't want to."

She handed her bag to Cynder on her way out. "Will you take this to my room at the club for me?"

"You got it." Cyn took the bag and then surprised Phyl by snaring her in a quick hug. "And whatever happens tonight, I hope you have fun."

"Me too." Fun, she could deal with. What might come after worried her. Garrett and Scott had broken her heart once. She would never let them do it again.

6

Scott checked the time again. "It's been more than five minutes."

"It's been six minutes and about seven seconds. I know because you keep informing me of the time in thirty-second increments. Relax, Scott. She'll be here soon."

"I am relaxed," Scott snapped. A second later he was laughing at himself. He was the farthest thing from relaxed right now. It was all he could do not to pace the corridor outside the *Beacon's* main door.

"Feel better now?" Garrett dropped a big hand onto his shoulder and squeezed lightly. "If she's taking time to get ready, that's a good thing. It means tonight matters to her."

"I do actually date, you know. Not often, but I remember how this goes. Mostly."

"Then why are you vibrating like you downed three shots of *ja'kreesh*?"

"Because this *matters*." Scott glanced at Garrett's hand, which was still on his shoulder. "Everything about tonight is important."

Garrett smiled, his mismatched eyes lighting up. "Yeah, it is. None of us are dumb kids anymore. We made a plan. If things get *fraxxed* up, we'll talk through it. This can work."

And that was the other issue. Over the last week, he'd spent a lot of time with Garrett. They'd met for planning sessions at the Nova Club every day. It wasn't long before the Nova crew had adopted Garrett as one of their own. Their planning sessions had turned into friendly meals and even a couple of sparring sessions down in the club's gym.

Whatever had been building between the two of them the last time they'd all been together hadn't gone away. It was still there, and this time there was no reason why they couldn't explore it. Garrett wasn't his subordinate anymore. He wasn't even military. They'd talked enough Scott knew that Garrett had long ago come to terms with his sexuality.

Back then, there had been all sorts of reasons why they hadn't acted on their attraction. Now there was only one—Phylomenia.

Bringing them all into the same orbit had been a tricky bit of piloting. Adding another variable might send all three off on different trajectories. Worse, it might mean that one of them got left behind. He didn't know which outcome worried him more.

Scott put his hand over Garrett's. "If this is going to work, you and I... we need to talk."

"Yeah?" Garrett's fingers relaxed beneath his.

"Yeah."

Garrett winked. "Good."

"Finally!" Phyl exclaimed, startling them both.

It was ironic that the one door on the *Beacon* that operated perfectly and silently was the one that allowed Phylomenia to join them without either of them noticing.

Scott jumped, Garrett pulled his hand away, and both of them turned to face their stealthy date.

Garrett whistled. "Damn, Mena. You still clean up nice."

"You look amazing." The dress was simple but elegant, leaving her legs bare to the knee. The fabric was either dark blue or black, he wasn't sure which. It was hard to tell because it seemed to shift and shimmer slightly as she moved. It took a moment for him to realize it wasn't an illusion. It was some sort of effect built into the fabric. Silver points of light reminded Scott of stars and moved like constellations across her svelte figure.

"Thank you, but don't change the subject. Did I hear what I think I did? Because I would have bet my ship that the stars would go dark long before the two of you figured things out."

"You knew?" Scott asked.

"That you two had a slow burn thing brewing? It was obvious from the moment I met you."

Garrett cleared his throat. "It wasn't obvious to me."

Phylomenia's laughter was light and silvery as she joined them and then reached up to pat Garrett's cheek. "I know, Gar-Bear."

"You haven't called me that in a long time." Garrett caught her hand in his and held it. "I like hearing it again."

"I figured if we're doing this, we might as well do it right." She turned to look at him. "Right, Scotty?"

"Absolutely. And it won't be right until I give you your last gift. Though it's more of a return than anything else."

He pulled the necklace from his pocket and held it out to her. Over the years, it had become a talisman of sorts. Some of the best days of his life had included the woman who'd worn it, and he'd kept it close at hand.

"You found it! I thought that was long gone." Phyl reached for it but then stopped, her fingers not quite touching the little heart-shaped memory crystal that dangled at the end of the chain.

"You kept it all this time?" she asked softly.

"I did, but it's time I gave it back to you." He undid the clasp. "May I?"

"Yes." Phyl's eyes were soft. "I never imagined you being the sentimental type."

Scott stayed quiet as he moved behind her and placed the pendant around her neck.

She tipped her head to one side, and it was the most natural thing in the galaxy for him to press a kiss to a spot beneath her ear as he fastened the chain.

"When it comes to you, Phylomenia Harrington, I will always be sentimental."

He was so close he couldn't miss her soft gasp or the subtle sway of her body as she moved closer to him.

This. This was what had been missing. He'd been going through the motions of courtship without letting himself feel anything. No wonder Phyl hadn't come back to him. She probably hadn't even noticed he was trying.

"Phyl..." he didn't know what to say next, so he nuzzled her neck again, breathing in the scent of her skin.

"We share. Remember?" Garrett said, his voice barely more than a distant rumble as he stepped in front of Phylomenia.

"Sorry. It's been a while since I've had to do that."

Scott raised his head only to have Garrett touch his cheek and then Phylomenia's. "For me, too."

"Me three. After the way we ended, I never..." Phyl shook her head sharply, her entire body going taut. "What the hell are we doing?"

Garrett smiled at them both, a bittersweet expression that made Scott's heart twist. He remembered that smile. It was the one Garrett had given him just before he'd walked away for the last time. Regret, affection, and frustration all rolled into one. "This is us correcting our course. The three of us should have been in each other's orbits all this time, but we *fraxxed* up. We might do it again, too. I'd rather crash and crater than spend the rest of my life wondering what could have been."

Scott reached around to tap the top of the pendant, and a small holo-projection shimmered into existence just in front of Phyl. It was an image of the three of them, arms wrapped around each other, young, in love, and laughing without a care in the world.

"It still works," Phyl murmured, watching the short clip play and then flicker away again.

"And so do we. We're not the same people we were back then. We're older and smarter," Scott said.

"And grayer," Phyl added.

"I like the gray. On both of you," Garrett said and pressed a kiss to Phyl's cheek with his eyes locked on Scott the whole time.

"Presents, flirting, and flattery. This evening is off to a fine start." Phyl took both he and Garrett by the hand. "For the record, I still think this is an insane idea. But... I thought that the last time, too. When it comes to the two of you, I seem to have a problem saying no."

"Then don't. We'll make it easy for you. Would you like to go to dinner now?" Scott asked.

"Yes," she replied.

"See? Easy. My turn. Would you do me the honor of dancing with me this evening?" Garrett asked.

Phyl laughed. "Also, yes."

"And then would you dance with me?" Scott asked.

She tipped her head to the side and pretended to consider her answer for several seconds.

"The word you're looking for is yes," he prompted her.

"Oh. Right." She grinned. "Yes, I'll dance with you."

"Good girl. For that, you get to pick dessert," Garrett said in a tone that made Scott's heart speed up. The bastard was right. He did like it when Garrett took charge of a situation, of Phylomenia, or even... he brushed that thought aside before it took form. Tonight was about winning their lady back.

"Two things wrong with that statement. One. I'm no girl. Two. You are not the boss of me."

Garrett turned sharply and caught hold of Phyl's waist with his free hand, pulling her in tightly. "Wrong. You are our girl. Always. And tonight, I am absolutely going to be the one calling the shots. And you're both going to let me."

Scott tightened his grip on Phyl's hand. He had no idea how she'd react to Garrett's statement. That hadn't been part of their plan.

"Garrett..." he growled in warning. If that damned

fool pushed Phylomenia too hard and ruined tonight, there'd be hell to pay.

"You've changed," was all Phyl said.

"And?" Garrett was still pushing.

"And I'll let you know what I think before we have dessert." She rose on her toes to kiss Garrett's cheek and then turned and smiled at him. "Come here, Scotty."

"You are not the boss of me, either," he joked but moved in close.

To his delight, Phyl kissed him on the cheek, too, without leaving Garrett's embrace. It was the closest he'd been to them both in decades, and *fraxx* did it feel right.

None of them moved or spoke for several long minutes.

"I've missed this," Phyl murmured softly.

"So have I," both he and Garrett said at the same time.

"I've missed that, too," she said.

Scott knew what she meant. There'd been a time the three of them had been so in synch with each other they often said the same thing at the same time or finished each other's sentences. He looked down at Phyl and then back up to Garrett. He wanted that feeling back, and this time, he'd find a way to keep it.

It dawned on Garrett that he'd spent the last week planning the perfect date while forgetting the first rule of combat. No plan survived long once the battle started.

He'd taken the lead, which meant now, he had to follow through and get them back on track. "Dinner awaits. Shall we?"

"We're walking?" Phyl asked.

"We are not. My job comes with perks. A transport and driver are waiting for us nearby," Scott said.

"You're making one of your soldiers drive us to dinner?"

"I'm not making anyone do anything," was all Scott said.

Garrett grinned to himself as he led them down the corridor. He knew who was driving, and it wasn't one of Scott's staff.

Their driver was waiting with the vehicle, snapping to attention like the soldier he'd been once.

"You? Are you all in on this?" Phyl demanded of the dark-haired cyborg who had volunteered to drive.

"It was a family effort," Ward said, grinning.

"Does this mean your batch-brother is around here somewhere, too?"

"Somewhere," Ward confirmed. "But I'm not going to spoil the surprise."

He opened the rear doors and gestured for them to climb in.

Garrett hadn't been in one of the transports before.

It was like a small-scale shuttle, only with a far plusher interior, purified air, and seats that formed around his body like a lover's touch. "Nice perk."

"One I rarely use," Scott said.

"Because you never leave your damn office. You have no idea what's really going on around here, Scotty."

Garrett raised a hand. "No."

"No?" Phyl repeated, her brows twitching as surprise and annoyance both tried to overtake her expression at the same time.

"No politics tonight and as little reality as possible."

"I'm not sure I like this new, bossier you."

He sat back and grinned as if he didn't have a care in the world. "You'll get used to it."

There was a short bark of strangled laughter from their driver, but before anyone could comment Ward had them airborne.

After a few seconds, Garrett decided it would be better not to watch as the cyborg sped along the roof of the main concourse, dodging ducts, pipes and the occasional sign.

Phylomenia kept hold of both their hands for the short journey, and he hated the need to let go of her as they exited.

The concourse was filled with throngs of beings from a variety of species and worlds. Off-duty soldiers mixed with low-level lackeys and a few miners and cargo crews who hadn't left the station yet. They would, though. Soon the station would be completely overrun by Tianna Astor's incoming guests.

He helped Phylomenia out of the transport and then waited for Scott to exit the far door and come around to join them.

"Where is everyone?" she asked and gestured to the empty space in front of Amped. The lights were on, but there was no line of patrons awaiting entry.

"Closed for a private function," she read a small sign posted on one door and then stopped walking. "Tell me you two didn't close down this whole place for our date. Times are tight. Everyone needs all the income they can get!"

"Easy, spitfire. It's all taken care of." Garrett had happily bought out every table for the night. He had more scrip than he could spend in several lifetimes, but he still remembered what it was like to have nothing. Now he had money, and he was generous with it.

A voice came from the shadows near the door, and Garrett instinctively reached for the blaster he wasn't currently wearing.

"Welcome to Amped," Victor said as he stepped into view.

"Assassins are annoyingly stealthy," Scott muttered.

"Ex-assassin, thank you. Tonight, I'm a doorman."

Phyl looked pointedly around them. "You're going to be a very bored one."

"Wolf and I will make sure you have a nice, quiet evening."

"That's sweet." Phyl grinned up at the cyborg and winked. "But the way this is going, I'm not sure nice is the right word to use. I'll let you know tomorrow."

For the first time in his life, Garrett saw a cyborg blush.

None of them said a word as Victor opened the door and let them in.

It was the first time he'd been inside. Dark paneled walls, high-backed chairs, and a deep red and gold color scheme gave the space a sense of elegance and intimacy. Light cubes glowed at every table, casting enough illumination he could make out dozens of pictures of musicians hanging on the walls.

"Hello. Your table is over this way," a redheaded human woman with a bright smile greeted them.

"They dragged you into this too, Lieksa?" Phyl asked.

"Hell no. I volunteered. I'll be your server tonight. Not to worry, Jinella and T'arv are in the kitchen, so the food will be amazing. I'm just delivering it."

"Where's the rest of the staff?" Phyl asked.

"They're getting the night off with full pay." Lieksa led them to a small, raised area just beside the stage. A single table had been set up with three place settings and a covered basket of what had to be fresh bread by the smell.

"They are?" Phyl glanced at him. "All taken care of. Huh?"

"I told you so." He allowed himself a moment of smugness.

"Don't encourage him, spitfire. I've had to spend the last week with him, and trust me, once he starts feeling cocky he gets annoyingly smug."

"Pot, meet kettle. Kettle, pot," Phyl said.

"I... have no idea what that means, but I think she just insulted both of us," Garrett said.

"I *do* know what that means, and yes, she did."

Lieksa waited until they were seated and then handed each of them a small, hand- written menu. "Tonight's meal is a set menu with a few variations to choose from. The first course is fresh greens tossed with a citrus dressing."

"Oranges? Please tell me it has orange juice in it." Phyl exclaimed.

"It does," Lieksa said with a wink.

"The main entrée is chicken scaloppine with mushrooms and your choice of several side dishes. The options are listed on your menu. I'll take your dessert order later, but for now, please enjoy your drinks. I'll be back with your wine in a moment and can take your orders for dinner then."

"This entire menu is a list of some of my favorite things." Phyl looked from Scott to him and back. "Did you two get anything else done this week?"

"We can multitask," Scott retorted.

"When we have to. Honestly, most of my week was supposed to be spent getting familiar with the station and figuring out how to keep my client safe. Between Scott going over the maps with me and your friends providing information and even guided tours, it didn't take me long to come up with my plans. Don't tell my client, but this might be the easiest job I've had in years."

"Who is your client any—Wait. Is this cherry cola?" Phyl raised her glass to her lips and took a sip. "It is. Okay, I'm officially starting to love this date."

"Told you," Scott said with a laugh.

"That stuff will rot your insides. I cannot believe you still drink it, Mena."

"The wonders of nanotech. I have the metabolism of a teenager, a cast iron stomach, and I laugh in the face of cholesterol. Also, no more hangovers."

"I miss my old metabolism," Scott broke off a piece of bread and slathered it in butter. "This meal is going to cost me three days in the gym."

Garrett wasn't sure that was true. In fact, he hoped that any calories they consumed at dinner would be burned off by morning... if Phylomenia said yes.

They were laughing and teasing each other by the time Lieksa returned with a bottle of wine and glasses.

The laughter carried on after she vanished into the kitchen with their orders.

The entertainment started as they ate their first course—hydroponically grown greens tossed in a dressing of citrus that elevated the simple dish to something quite extraordinary. While they were enjoying the food, a soft strumming came from the still-darkened stage.

They all turned to look as lights came on slowly, revealing a dark-haired giant of a man seated on a stool with a guitar in his hands.

"Holy *fraxx*. You asked Mack to sing for us?" Phylomenia asked.

Garrett took her hand. "I didn't have to ask. They volunteered. Every single one of them wanted to be part of this. They helped us plan, told us all your favorite things, and offered up their time, all for you."

"They wanted to make this night special for you because they adore you," Scott said as he took her other hand.

"They also made it clear that if we hurt you again, our bodies would never be found," Garrett added.

"We had almost as many threats as offers to help. As families go, spitfire, you found yourself one of the best." It was high praise coming from Scott, and they both knew it, but his words stung, too. There'd been a time when he and Scott were Phylomenia's family. He was going to do his damnedest to make that happen again.

Mack played and sang softly as they ate. When the first course was cleared away, Garrett stood and offered Phyl his hand. "Dance with me?"

She smiled up at him but didn't move. "Not with you, no."

That set him back. "No? You already agreed to dance with me."

"I did. But if we're going to do this, I intend to do it right from the beginning. I'd like to dance with *both* of you."

"Ah. In that case..." He held out his free hand to Scott. "Care to dance with us?"

Scott didn't hesitate. The moment their hands touched, something clicked deep in Garrett's soul. They moved to an open area beside their table. There was enough light to see, but the three of them were wrapped in partial shadow as they came together.

Garrett drew Phylomenia into his arms and Scott stepped in behind her, the three of them wrapping their arms around each other to dance to the slow beat of Mack's song.

Holding on to the two people who had once meant everything to him, Garrett couldn't help but wonder how the *fraxx* he'd been stupid enough to walk away. At the time, he'd been sure it was the only thing he could do. Looking back, he wasn't so certain. They'd let secrets and doubts tear their trio apart once. This time, he wouldn't walk away so fast... Hell, he wasn't sure he could walk away at all.

Things were different now. He wasn't a brash kid anymore. He was a grown man who was used to getting what he wanted. There was another difference, too.

This time, he was the one with the secret. How would they react if he told them the truth? He wasn't a corporate lackey. He was a deep cover IAF spy and had been since the day he'd left. If this was going to work, he'd have to tell them eventually. But if he did... would they forgive him, or would history repeat itself?

7

IT HAD BEEN YEARS SINCE SHE'D DANCED WITH A man, never mind two. Phylomenia was grateful that it was a slow, easy song that let her enjoy being close to Scott and Garrett without having to recall how to actually dance.

The empty room made it easier to enjoy the moment. No one was here to see them. No risk of gossip getting back to Scott's forces or Garrett's clients about what the three of them were doing.

The need for discretion had been a constant source of friction between them last time. It wasn't a problem at first, but as their relationship had deepened, so had the pressure. A woman casually seeing two men was one thing, especially when she wasn't military. When they'd become a trio, perceptions had changed, and not everyone was accepting.

She hadn't cared much, but Scott had. Once he got promoted, he'd worried about appearances to the point they almost never went out. Whenever her work as a courier brought her to the station, their dates almost always started out as a meal somewhere and ended in a hotel room.

The memory made her laugh. Thirty years later and here they were again—together in relative secrecy and nowhere to go but a hotel room afterward... or her ship. Her bed on the Beacon was nothing more than a standard bunk, though. It was the perfect size for her and her alone, and that's how she liked it.

"It's good to hear you laugh again. I missed that sound." Garrett leaned in and brushed a tender kiss to her lips. "I missed you, Mena."

It would have been easy to challenge him or remind him that he'd left her. She didn't. One thing life had taught her—the only way to leave the past behind was not to think about it too much. If you did, it became a freeloading passenger tainting every new experience.

"We're here, now. That's more than I ever thought we'd have," she said.

She didn't know which of them moved first, but between one heartbeat and another everything changed. Scott pressed in behind her, his solid form pushing her up against Garrett. Someone's fingers stroked over the back of her neck and then up to cradle her head in one big hand as Garrett kissed her a second time.

Heat washed over her as his mouth claimed hers and she closed her eyes, falling into this moment like light plunging into a black hole. The moment she'd seen him, she'd known this was the most likely outcome. She could have kept one of them at a distance, but not both. Not when they worked together the way they were tonight.

Her fingers tangled in the front of Garrett's shirt, pulling him in closer as she kissed him back. Archer's mouth was on her neck, nibbling up to her ear and whispering all the wicked things he wanted to do to her.

She reached back, found the waistband of his pants and hung tightly to him, pulling them both in close.

When Scott nipped at her earlobe, she moaned, the sound captured by Garrett's mouth. He took advantage of the moment to sweep his tongue into her mouth, dominating her while Scott kept up his barrage of whispers.

"I'm going to kiss you and then taste you. Strip you naked and listen to you scream while Garrett takes his turn. All you have to do is say yes, spitfire. I have missed you so *fraxxing* much. I need you to say yes."

Need flowed through her like molten steel, but she kept her silence. Her answer was obvious to all of them. No need to make it official yet.

"Tease," Garrett whispered against her mouth. "We'll make you pay for that later."

"Is that a threat or a promise?"

Both men groaned, a low, needy sound she felt as much as heard.

"Which would you like it to be?" Scott asked.

"Can it be both?" she asked.

Scott growled, and a moment later she'd been spun around so she was facing him instead of Garrett. "Both sounds good to me."

Then he kissed her.

She'd spent months convincing herself that she could just be friends with Scott. That lie went up in flames the moment his mouth crashed down on hers.

"Oh, yes. I have missed this," Garrett murmured. His hard body and even harder cock pressed up against her back as she clung to Scott, kissing him back with a hunger that threatened to burn her to ashes where she stood.

They kissed and caressed each other until nothing in the universe remained except the three of them. She was so lost in the moment she almost missed the soft footfalls coming up the stairs.

Lieksa had returned to remove their plates, and none of them had noticed until she was only a few steps away.

"Dinner. We should get back to it," she suggested, feeling slightly foolish at being caught.

"The only thing I want to eat right now is—"

She turned and kissed Garrett to stop him from finishing that sentence.

They moved apart and drifted back to the table, still holding hands.

"Behave. Both of you," she said in a hushed whisper. "We've already given the kids an eyeful. Don't need them overhearing anything that will put them in therapy."

Mack mangled the next note of his song as he struggled to control his laughter.

"Damned cyborg hearing!" Phylomenia didn't bother whispering this time.

Mack stopped playing and looked up, an ear-to-ear grin on his face. "Sorry, Phyl. Can't help it. Part of the design."

Lieksa giggled and zipped past them, her hands full of empty dishes. "Be right back with the next course."

Mack went back to his playing, picking out a lively tune that made Phylomenia smile. "I haven't heard that one in... well, longer than I care to admit."

"Me either," Garrett said. "Didn't they used to play this at the bar—what the hell was it called?"

"Brass Tactics," Scott said. "It was still in operation the last time I was back there. Same cheap beer and greasy food."

"They had the best ice cream sundaes, though. Do you remember?" They'd taken her there one night and nearly eaten themselves into a coma devouring the largest sundae she'd ever seen. The three of them hadn't been able to finish it, and she'd sworn off ice cream for six months afterward.

Lieksa brought out their entrées while they waxed nostalgic, talking about beings and places they'd known back then. They laughed, ate, and drank until the bottle and their plates were empty.

She sipped the last of her cherry cola and smiled as Lieksa arrived with another menu.

"Desserts," she announced, her smile almost wicked as she handed Phylomenia the card. "I was informed it would be the lady's choice."

Phylomenia scanned it quickly and then read it again, more slowly this time.

Option one was a chocolate torte, and option two was a cherry trifle—both favorites of hers and both quite normal. However, the third option gave her pause. No dessert was listed, just a note that said, "Say yes and see."

"I don't know what to choose! I love chocolate, and trifle is always a nice way to end a meal." She tapped her finger against her lips. "This is a tough choice."

"Spitfire..." Scott growled, but his eyes were dancing as he took her hand from her mouth and held it. "You did tell Garrett you'd tell him what you thought of the new him before dessert. I think you've left us both in suspense long enough."

"You're right. I have." She set the menu down. "I can answer that question and order dessert at the same time. I choose the third option. To go, if possible."

Lieksa bounced in place and beamed. "Oh, it definitely is. In fact..." She set two fingers to her mouth and whistled sharply.

Mack stopped playing, and a moment later the stool he'd been perched on was empty. The stage lights flicked off, and someone, Phylomenia thought it sounded like Dash, whooped from the kitchen.

"I should have known that one wasn't far off," Phylomenia muttered.

"He was watching the back door and taste testing the food," Lieksa joked. "Gentlemen, option three is waiting for you outside. Have a wonderful evening."

"Thank you for being part of it. Tell everyone thank you."

The little redhead grinned and darted in for a quick hug. "Be happy, Phyl. That's all we want for you." Then she turned her attention to Garrett and Scott. "I don't need to remind you what happens if she isn't happy. Right?"

"No need to repeat yourself. We'll take care of her," Garrett said, rising.

"You better." Lieksa descended the stairs and waited, clearly intending on escorting them out.

They followed her.

Victor was waiting for them at the door. "Ward will be here in a few minutes. Stay inside until he lands."

"Problems?" Scott asked.

"Nothing major. There was a rally earlier, a few of the locals getting riled up about the current state of the station. It's over now, but a few of the more agitated ones are still around, looking for trouble."

"I know we're not talking about this tonight, Scotty, but we need to. Soon," Phylomenia said. She'd been worried this would happen. Then she let the topic go and focused on the immediate future. "Where are we going? Please tell me it's not to the same sorts of places we used to go when we were kids."

"It's not. Back then, you and I were broke, and Scott was too cheap to spend any of his money on us. Now, things are different. We're going to my hotel." Garrett pointed upward. "The California."

It was the most exclusive, expensive hotel on the station. "Damn. Do you think they'll let me in? I mean..." She gestured to herself. "I'm not exactly their usual clientele."

"A long time ago, a young officer shared a secret with me. He was an uppity ass, but the kind that sort of grew on you."

"Asshole," Scott growled. "I wasn't uppity. And there were reasons I couldn't pay for things back then."

"Are you going to let me finish my story?"

Scott waved him on, but Phylomenia saw the tension lines around his mouth. This wasn't the time to have that conversation, but it would have to happen soon.

"What did this fine young officer tell you, Gar-Bear?" she asked.

"So long as you acted like you had every right to be there, most people would assume you did and never question it."

"Good advice." It was the way she lived her life for the most part, though usually it was because she was walking into notorious places full of dangerous beings.

This wouldn't be so different, though this time, the danger wouldn't be waiting for her. It was coming with her in the form of the only men she'd ever really loved.

Scott tried to brush it off, but Garrett's barb about him being cheap still rankled. There was more to it than either of them knew. One day, he'd have to tell them. He should have done it thirty years ago. Maybe that would have changed things between them.

Maybe.

Their transport landed and Victor escorted them to the vehicle. Ward hopped out to open the doors, and both of them wore identically pleased expressions.

Phylomenia took one look inside and laughed. "Those little minxes."

The bag she'd given to Cynder sat on the floor. Scott knew it had been repacked with everything she might need for an overnight stay. Cyn and Zura had seen to it.

If Phyl had made another choice, the bag would have been stashed out of sight and returned to Zura later. He was gratified that wouldn't happen. At least, not if they could hold on to the magic of this moment.

Ward took them on a convoluted route that allowed them to traverse the length of the station while moving up levels. It was an impressive bit of navigation. If he ever needed to get around the station in a hurry, he'd have to remember to bring one of the cyborgs with him. Not that he expected to need to, but he hadn't lived as long as he had by assuming things would never go wrong.

Their destination was inaccessible by transport, so Ward delivered them to a bank of mag-levs that would take them up to the final level. Corp-Sec officers stood guard at several key points, watching the steady flow of beings coming and going from the lifts.

To call the mag-lev for their level, Garrett had to identify himself and submit to a palm scan. The security feature had one purpose—to keep out the riff-raff.

"Funny. I don't recall seeing any security on the lower floors. Or locked mag-levs either," Phylomenia said.

"Mena, you promised. No reality tonight. You can get back on the warpath tomorrow," Garrett said.

"Right. Sorry." Their little spitfire actually looked regretful for a full three seconds before glancing his way. "We'll talk about it later."

Scott knew exactly how to get them back on the right track. Only the three of them were in the mag-lev when the doors closed, and the moment they were alone, he had Phylomenia up against the side of the lift, one arm locked around her waist with his thigh between her knees. "You're thinking too much. Let me fix that for you."

He dropped his mouth to hers and kissed her until she softened in his arms. Her lips parted with a low hum of approval, her arms twining round his neck as she kissed him back. She nipped at his lower lip until his cock was hard enough to hammer through hull plating and his blood was pounding in his ears.

That's when Garrett joined in, sliding his arm around Scott's waist as he fit himself between them. Phyl moaned and quivered in Scott's arms, and he let her soft sounds roll through him, drinking in the taste and feel of her like it was his last moment of existence.

Scott lifted his head, giving Garrett space to kiss Phyl, but that's not what happened. Garrett turned toward him, their eyes locked, and they both went still.

Time stretched out like taffy. Neither moved, and then suddenly they came together in a kiss that was far more tentative than the ones he'd been giving Phylomenia.

He tried to hang on to the details of this moment. The coarse prickle of beard, the scent of sandalwood and citrus, Garrett's rough rumble of desire as their mouths met. Being with Garrett like this was new territory.

He didn't get more than a moment to enjoy it either because a soft chime announced they'd reached their level.

"The mag-lev has lousy timing," Garrett grumbled.

"Extremely." Phylomenia sounded as nonplussed as he felt.

"You liked watching us, Mena?" Garrett asked softly as they stepped out onto the station once more.

"Hell yes. I'm starting to see the appeal of being a voyeur."

Scott was grateful he'd worn a longer, loose sweater that hid his current state of arousal. Garrett carried Phyl's bag, the strap slung over one shoulder so he could hide the tent in his pants.

"Now we all look equally disreputable," Phyl announced with glee and took them each by the hand.

The air was purified and lightly fragranced to smell of something that reminded him of summer evenings planet-side. The broad concourse was made to look vaguely like a street, down to the cobblestone pattern in the flooring and light cubes set on columns to look like streetlamps.

Phyl looked around with wide eyes. "Was that a mag-lev or a wormhole to another dimension? This does not look like the same station we were on two minutes ago."

"For all intents and purposes, it isn't. This is what

money and power buys you, even out here." Garrett gestured around them and then pointed toward a large glass doorway. "And there's the hotel. I think it's time we went somewhere with a locking door. Don't you?"

No one bothered to answer. They didn't need to. They all knew what they wanted.

The lobby managed to be both ostentatious and understated at the same time with carpets so plush there was almost no sound as they walked across it. It also boasted faux stonework walls, high-backed chairs, and carved tables so dark and well-polished they might have been actual wood. Even an open fountain of real water burbled in the center.

"That's more water than a family of four is allotted in a week," Phyl mentioned as they passed the fountain. "And I know I promised. It's just difficult to wrap my head around."

"Which is why they don't let many beings see it for themselves. Rumors are one thing, but if the general population knew this existed..." Garrett shrugged.

"Nothing good would come of it," Phylomenia agreed. "But when in the history of everything has hiding the truth ever worked out for long?"

All three of them fell quiet. Phylomenia had inadvertently reminded them all that secrets were part of the reason they'd gone their separate ways.

This hotel was run entirely by droids and holographic interfaces. Everything was automated to allow for as much privacy and convenience as possible for the guests.

A touch of his palm was all it took for the mag-lev to take them to the correct floor. Only a handful of doors lined the hallway, and Garrett led them to the one farthest from the elevator.

"Welcome to my current home," he said and waved his hand over yet another palm reader. The door slid open with barely a whisper, and they fell back as Phylomenia entered first.

"Definitely an improvement from the old days." He heard a rare note of awe in their spitfire's voice.

The lobby might have been ostentatious, but the suite itself was a study in subtle luxury with soft lines, elegant furnishings, and a viewport that spanned most of the outer wall. Countless stars gleamed brightly in the darkness. It made Scott itch to be back in the pilot's seat again. These days, the only times he was even on his private ship was to use it as a second, more secure office. If the bed had been bigger, he'd have suggested using it for this tryst. But he had to admit, Garrett's hotel room was far nicer.

Phyl walked straight to the viewport to stare at the stars. "Do you miss it, Gar?"

They joined her, one on each side, both with an arm draped around her waist. Their arms nestled against each other.

"Which part?" Garrett asked.

"Flying out in the big black. Nothing but the void and the stars for company."

"Sometimes. But the price was too high. I was never going to make it as a career officer. I didn't have the temperament."

"Too stubborn," Scott said, turning his hand so it was resting lightly on Garrett's arm.

"True. And I was never good at taking orders." Garrett leaned back to look at him. "Even after all the time and work you've put in, you still have to take orders sometimes. Doesn't it rankle?"

"Sometimes," Scott admitted. "But I still believe in the work." He dropped a kiss to the top of Phyl's head. "Though at times I think you were the smartest of us all, spitfire. You're still flying your own ship by your own rules."

"My ship's older than I am, and these days I fly for Zura. She doesn't have a lot of rules, but I'm not my own boss anymore." She shrugged and leaned back into their embrace. "But my cargo is mostly legal, and no one has threatened to arrest me in a year, so... that's nice."

"A year? That's it? What the hell were you doing before?" Garrett demanded.

"The same thing I've been doing since I left. Running cargo. The kind it's best not to know much about. Though I never had anything to do with hard pharma or slavery of any kind. Other than that? I did what I needed to." She turned and looked at Garrett. "Just like you."

"And that's enough talking for tonight," Scott announced. He stepped away from the two of them and deliberately skinned his top over his head. It was an obvious distraction but a necessary one. Plenty had changed since the last time they'd been together, but one thing never would. The three of them in one room were like trying to bottle lightning. Eventually something would crack and there would be an explosion.

"You know, I like the view outside, but the one in here is even better," Phylomenia drawled, her accent thick as honey.

By the time he had his shirt off and could see again, Phylomenia was leaning against the window, her long legs crossed over each other and a predatory smile on her face.

"You are beautiful, Phyl. Starlight becomes you."

"You're kinda pretty yourself, Scotty. I don't remember you having that many muscles the last time I saw you naked."

He flexed like a teenager trying to impress his first girlfriend. "I've been training with the Nova Club crew. It's humbling but effective."

"Truth. I haven't had my ass handed to me that fast since basic training." Garrett walked straight for him, bringing Phylomenia with him. "It looks good on you, Scott."

"You know what would look even better? Both of you shirtless. Since it appears there is no dessert on offer tonight, I'll have to make do with enjoying the two of you."

Garrett's voice dropped to a low rumble that made Phyl's cheeks heat and Scott's cock twitch. Damn, that man had a voice made for sinning. "We can call room service, but I already know what I'm having... and it's not on the menu. Scott, you ready to have dessert?"

"You know it."

"Then I think you should help the lady with her dress while I fulfill her request." It wasn't worded as an order, but there was no missing the tone of command in Garrett's voice.

For once, Scott was happy not to be the one in charge. He spent all his time telling other people what to do. Tonight, he was taking some time off with two of the people who mattered the most in his life, even if they'd been missing for more than half of it.

8

This was happening.

Phylomenia glanced at her bag sitting not far from the door and allowed herself a moment to envision what would happen if she decided to leave. In her mind, she didn't even reach the door.

She didn't want to go, which probably meant she was even crazier than advertised and destined for yet another round of heartbreak. So be it. She'd taken bigger risks in her life and survived, and another night with these two would be worth it. She knew that much already. They'd been good together back in the day.

She'd bet a month's income they'd be better this time around.

Scott moved behind her, warm hands undoing the fastenings on her dress and smoothing it off her shoulders. "You are so beautiful."

"Liar. Save the flattery for Garrett. I wasn't then, and I'm certainly not now."

His teeth closed on the top of her shoulder in a light nip. "Stop arguing, dammit. I think you're beautiful. I always have." He kissed the same spot he'd nipped a moment ago. "I always will."

Garrett stood in front of her, stripping out of his clothes with slow, deliberate movements. His gaze never left the two of them, and Phyl was as entranced by the primal moves of the man in front of her as by the whispered compliments from the one behind.

Heat pooled deep in her belly, her breasts aching with the need to be touched. Her clit throbbed, and her skin was suddenly so sensitive that the slightest touch felt like fire racing across her flesh.

She pulled her arms out of her sleeves and let the dress slide down her body to pool at her feet.

"Fraxx!" Garrett swore.

"Spitfire... why aren't you wearing underwear?" Scott's voice was a husky rasp near her ear, his hands smoothing down her body to rest on her bare hips.

"The girls didn't pack me any."

"You've been naked..." Garrett growled, tearing off his pants with none of his previous calm.

"All this time?" Scott finished Garrett's sentence.

"I was dressed. If I were naked, there's no way I'd have been allowed on that mag-lev."

"Minx!" Garrett was on her in an instant, his mouth hard and hot as he slanted his lips over hers. His beard rasped her cheeks, the friction adding to the heat generated by his demanding kiss.

She was caught between them, bare skin pressing in from both sides. It was exactly where she wanted to be—caught in a vise of muscle and heat. Rising on her toes, she kissed Garrett back, her hand moving up his body to settle on the curve of one powerful shoulder while she also reached down to cover Scott's hand where it rested on her hip.

Her senses spun and whirled and her heart was pounding as she held on to the two of them, lost in a storm of sensations. Scott slid his free hand up her flank, working his way between her and Garrett until he could palm one breast. He was still partially dressed, but she could feel the hard ridge of his erection pressed against her ass through his pants.

Moaning loudly, she opened her mouth to Garrett. She needed more. Touch. Taste. Them. Everything.

Scott kissed his way up her shoulder and along the side of her neck until his breath was a soft caress against her ear. She shivered in delight at the sensual pleasure of it, her pussy getting slicker by the second. Wordlessly she shifted position, opening her legs so Garrett's thigh was between hers and giving her something to grind herself against as she tried to ease the throbbing ache of her clit.

"Need something?" Scott asked a bare second before his lips found her earlobe and he sucked on it gently.

"For the love of gravity, yes. I need you. Both of you. Now."

Garrett's chuckle was low and rich with satisfaction. "As the lady wishes."

They both stepped back, which was not at all what she'd been hoping for. Then Garrett took her hands in his and kissed her softly. "Come with me."

She paused just long enough to kick off her shoes and then followed after him. The bedroom door was already open, and it was as opulent and spacious as the rest of his suite. It even had its own viewport, and the glow of millions of stars added their illumination to several light cubes that gave off just enough light to see.

The light cast shadows over Garrett's body, defining the cut of his muscles and highlighting the silver in his hair.

The bed was larger than her entire cabin on the *Beacon*. All four bedposts extended two feet above the mattress and were made of some kind of burnished metal that matched the headboard. It looked sleek, modern, and decadent.

"Nice. Which corner of this vast expanse do you actually sleep in?"

"All of it. Because I can." Garrett winked at her. "But tonight, I plan on sleeping right beside you."

"And I'll be on the other side," Scott announced. He strode into the room naked and as confident as ever, his silver hair gleaming in the starlight.

No doubt time had been good to both her former

lovers. Anti-aging treatments helped, of course, and both of them had the money to buy the best. The changes in their appearances only added to their sense of gravitas and experience. Not that she was going to tell them that.

"Scott. Her hands," Garrett said.

"My pleasure."

"What about my hands?" she demanded. But Scott had her by the wrists, drawing her hands together in front of her.

The bracelets on her wrists vibrated suddenly, coming together with a surprising amount of force. She pulled at her wrists. Nothing happened.

Mag cuffs. Her pretty presents were actually remotely activated mag-cuffs.

"You sons of—" she didn't get to finish her insult before Scott cut her off with a kiss so hot she swore the air started to sizzle.

"Perfect. Now, bed. Arms over your head if you please, spitfire," Garrett said.

She lifted her hands and flashed an obscene gesture at Garrett over Scott's shoulder.

The move left her open, though, and Scott took the advantage, picking her up and carrying her over to the bed. When she reached for him, he caught her wrists in one hand, guiding them toward the headboard.

She realized the plan a moment too late, and the cuffs locked onto the metal headboard with a crisp *click*.

"What's the point of all this?" she demanded.

"Pleasure, mostly," Scott murmured as he settled in beside her.

"And insurance that you don't leave until morning. Or did you think we'd forgotten your habit of slipping out before dawn?" Garrett added. He was standing next to the bed now, one hand fisting his cock as he stared down at her with satisfaction and desire.

"That was a long time ago. And I had a job to do. Getting an early start was necessary."

"It was last week," Scott said, tweaking one of her nipples.

She huffed and squirmed. "If I promise not to leave until the dayshift, will you undo these cuffs?"

"Gifts. The word you're looking for is gifts, spitfire. Our gifts to you."

"You gave me cuffs. I'm still working out how I feel about that." The truth was that neither bracelet was tight enough to keep her bound if she wanted to escape. She could have her hands free in a few seconds, which was why she wasn't angry. This was playtime, and she was happy to take part.

"They're very pretty cuffs," Scott pointed out.

"For a very pretty lady."

Phyl quirked an eyebrow. "You just bound me to the bed. Do better than pretty."

Garrett strolled down to the end of the bed, positioned himself at her feet, and stared for a few seconds. "Gorgeous. Legs to die for. Sexy. Frustrating.

Beautiful. Stubborn. You are the gold standard for every woman and man I've dated since we parted, and none of them have ever come close to matching you, Phylomenia Harrington."

He released his cock and then leaned down to wrap his hands around her ankles, spreading her legs wider before kneeling between them. His eyes gleamed like a predator as he moved up the bed to settle between her thighs.

Scott was toying with her breasts, fingers stroking and pinching by turns, his cock bumping against her hip as he teased her.

"I think you might want to hold on to something, spitfire. He looks like a man with a plan."

She banged her cuffs against the smooth metal of the headboard. "Hang on to what?"

Both of them laughed, the sound rolling through her like music.

"Good point. Plan B, then. Lie back and let us show you how much we missed you." Scott skimmed a hand down her body, over the pillowy mound of her stomach and down to her thigh. He caught hold of her leg and drew it upward, baring her to Garrett's gaze.

"Thank you. You read my mind." Garrett draped her free leg over his shoulder and then dropped his mouth to her pussy.

The intensity of the contact nearly brought her off the bed. Strong fingers parted her labia as his tongue swept over her most sensitive flesh. He drew her clit into the heat of his mouth, working it with the tip of his tongue until Phylomenia moaned.

"That's right, spitfire. Tell us how good it feels. Then imagine how much better it's going to be when he slides a finger inside you," Scott said and then kissed her so hard she was pressed down into the mattress.

Garrett took his cue from Scott and pressed a long finger inside her. It felt so good she almost came, but she didn't let it happen. She wanted this to last.

"Stubborn," Garrett muttered and added another finger, pumping her with them as he licked and lashed at her clit.

She was stretched out between them, hands still bound as they unleashed a sensual assault. Fingers and mouths touched and teased, stroking and pleasuring her until she was panting and wild, teetering on the brink of orgasm.

Scott raised his head, breaking their kiss so he could stare into her eyes. "Come for us."

She did.

Pleasure shattered her like crystal struck with a golden hammer. Her cries were captured by Scott's next kiss as Garrett groaned, the vibration adding another layer of sensation as she bucked her hips against his mouth.

Her last thought as she floated up into the stratosphere of bliss was that this wasn't like the last time they'd been together. It was even better.

Garrett was almost drunk from the pleasure of this moment. The three of them were together again, and while they weren't the same people they'd been back then, the chemistry they had burned hotter than ever.

He wanted nothing more than to bury himself balls deep inside Mena and lay claim to her, but he held back. Scott hadn't tasted more than her mouth yet. It was time to rectify that.

The remote for her cuffs was on the bedside table, out of his reach but well within Scott's. Garrett pushed himself back to his knees, wiping his beard with the back of his hand. "Shall we let her up now?"

Scott winked at him and then looked down at their captive lover. "Do you promise not to vanish before morning, Phyl?"

"Does morning include breakfast and copious amounts of decadent coffee made with real cream and coffee beans?"

"It does."

"Then I'm staying. In fact, I might move in. Living at the club is safe and fun, but it's also noisy and crowded."

Scott tapped the remote and Phyl's cuffs deactivated, freeing her hands.

The first thing she did was take off the bracelets and place them on the same table as the remote. "Just in case anyone gets any ideas... I want to be an active participant from now on."

That's what he wanted, too. All of them together. Garrett looked over at Scott and exhaled sharply as he saw the look of desire in the other man's eyes. They both wanted Phylomenia, but this time they were both ready to admit they wanted each other, too.

"Feel like riding tonight, spitfire?" he asked.

"Hell yes." Phyl sat up, her hand landing in the center of Scott's chest. "Down, boy."

Scott flopped onto his back, grinning from ear to ear. "Yes, ma'am."

"Oh, I like this game already," Phylomenia crowed. She threw one leg over Scott's hips, straddling him and giving Garrett a breathtaking view of her bare back bathed in starlight.

His cock throbbed and his fingers itched with the need to stroke her skin and explore every inch of her, renewing his memories and adding in new details, like the scars that hadn't been there before and a faded tattoo of a blue rose on her shoulder.

"I'm liking it too. Care to take the lead for a moment, Mena?"

If humans were capable of purring, he was certain she'd have done so. Phylomenia turned to smile at him, as regal as any queen. "I thought you'd never ask. There's something I have always wanted to see but never thought I would."

She crooked a finger at him and then pointed to a spot next to Scott's shoulder.

"You're just trying to find a way to stop me from whispering dirty things in your ear while I fuck you," Scott said.

Garrett took that as permission, ignoring the banter between his two lovers as he moved higher up the bed. Without a word he gathered up most of the pillows and then waited for Scott to raise himself up so Garrett could use them to prop him up.

At least the pillows were fluffy enough not to give away the fact his hands shook.

Phylomenia leaned down to kiss Scott, using the motion to rise up and position herself over his cock.

Garrett reached in and helped, drawing a hiss of pleasure from Scott as his fingers curled around his dick for a brief second before Phyl took him inside.

"*Fraxx.* That's. Yes," Scott said and then closed his eyes and groaned.

Phyl kissed him again and then straightened up, one hand on Scott's chest as she rocked over him.

"Kiss me, Gar-Bear."

"With pleasure." He was already on his knees, so it was easy to lean in and claim her lips in another slow kiss. She settled one hand on his shoulder, nails pricking at his skin as she used him for both leverage and balance.

"Beautiful," Scott groaned from below them.

A moment later a strong hand wrapped around

Garrett's cock, working it with hard motions that made Garrett's hips jerk.

He moved without thinking, his mouth still mated to Phylomenia's as he shifted his body closer to Scott.

A hot tongue swirled over the crown of his dick and he groaned in encouragement.

This was what he'd dreamed of.

Phyl's kisses were hot and hungry, her tongue dancing with his in time to the rocking of her hips. And Scott... *veth*. Scott's talented tongue and strong fingers were going to turn him inside out soon.

Phyl's nails dug deeper into his shoulder and her next moan came with a breathy little catch he remembered. It meant she was close.

He slid one hand down to her hip, moving slowly and not bothering to look as he navigated by touch down to where she was joined with Scott. He found the button of her clit and started rubbing, adding the friction of his fingers to their lovemaking.

Both of his lovers groaned in tandem, the vibration buzzing against his mouth and cock at the same moment. It was exquisite torture. His control cracked, his hips jerking in an unsteady rhythm.

Phylomenia rode Scott hard, grinding herself against cock and fingers, her breasts bouncing as she threw back her head and cried out with pleasure.

Garrett felt her orgasm hit. Her body tightened around Scott's shaft as she shuddered once, twice, and then a third time.

"Mena," he growled her name. She turned to him, a cat-with-the-cream look on her face as she kissed him again.

Scott came next, his back bowing so high he lifted Phylomenia off the bed for a moment. His groans hummed against Garrett's cock, making his balls tighten.

Three heartbeats later Garrett came hard and Scott milked him with hard pumps of his fist as the three of them shuddered and moaned through their releases.

"Holy *fraxx*. I guess we're not too old for this after all," Phylomenia quipped as she slumped onto Scott's chest with a contented sigh.

"You had doubts?" Garrett gently tousled Scott's hair before withdrawing.

"About me? Nope. I've got medi-bots. You two, though..." Phyl trailed off with a smirk.

"I think she just insulted us, Gar."

"Oh, I know she did." Garrett flopped onto the bed beside them, one arm and one leg thrown over the pair. "Pretty daring, given she's already promised not to leave until after breakfast. Plenty of time to show her what she can do with her doubts..."

"All night long," Scott agreed.

It was the best idea he'd heard in ages. He wanted nothing more in the universe than to spend the night with his lovers, doing anything and everything but sleep.

9

Scott checked the time. Five minutes until his next appointment, and if he knew Tianna, she'd be exactly thirty seconds late. Late, because she was an Astor, a woman so rich and powerful she could set her schedule and never have anyone remark on it. Thirty seconds exactly because she was also a cyborg and always knew the precise time.

For once, he was happy to indulge her little power play. It gave him a few more seconds to sit back and take a break. He'd spent the morning delegating new tasks and reading over reports from his staff. One of the advantages of his position was the ability to hand off the day-to-day tasks to his subordinates so he could focus on the bigger issues of the moment. Right now that included the upcoming gala and the addition of a new military base to the Drift. Both projects were important to the stability of the region and this part of the galaxy as a whole.

The announcement of the new military base on the Drift would mean that in a few months, the IAF presence on Astek station would drop to almost nothing. It would go back to being a place for recreation while the new station housed a much larger, more robust fleet and military presence.

The ability to delegate also left him free to spend his evenings and his nights with his lovers without compromising his duties. It was a balancing act he wasn't well-practiced in. Normally duty came first, and he arranged the rest of his life around it. He couldn't do that this time. Phylomenia and Garrett deserved better. He just wasn't sure he could give it to them.

His career was all he had. It was the only part of his life he could be certain that everything he had, he'd earned with hard work and loyalty. He almost never touched the money from his family trust. At one time he'd used it to help his sister make ends meet, but she hadn't needed his help in years. Celeste had walked away from their family and carved her own path through life.

He was proud of her choice, but she'd left him to face the consequences of her actions. After she left, his parents' focus intensified on their remaining child. There were more rules. More expectations. More pressure to excel.

The military hadn't been their first choice for him,

but it was on their list of approved careers so they'd relented, eventually. He'd signed up as soon as he came of age. It was the only option that gave him the chance to leave home and escape his family's control.

Until Phylomenia and Garrett came back into his orbit, he'd thought this job was all he'd ever have. For the first time, he was wondering if there might be another option.

He was still pondering possibilities when the system announced his next appointment had arrived, twenty-nine seconds late.

"Send them in."

Tianna strode in with her two husbands only a few steps behind. Royan was grinning, Owen was groaning, and their lovely wife looked like she was ready to throttle them both. He knew that expression well. He'd seen it on Phyl's face often enough.

Scott got to his feet and greeted them as if he hadn't noticed the byplay. "Good to see you. I appreciate you taking the time to meet me here."

As he spoke, he set a privacy shield generator on the desk and activated it. Within seconds they were all encased inside a shimmering bubble no listening device could get through.

"If you come to me, there will be talk you're in my pocket." Tianna waved her hand as she sat down. "Making me come to you suggests we're on somewhat level footing. I mean, as much as we can be considering I own this entire station."

Scott didn't react. He just sat, stony faced, until all three of them dropped their masks and relaxed.

"Sorry," Royan said after a moment. "Lately we seem to be spending all our time pretending Owen and I are charming but harmless while Tianna embraces the role of corporate ice queen." He dropped into another chair with a dramatic sigh. "I mean, I *am* charming, but I'm far from harmless."

Tianna looked at her two men with affection and then focused back on Scott. "Speaking of pretenses. Any luck finding out who your mole is?"

Scott grimaced. "Not yet. My operatives have narrowed it down, but the list is still longer than I'd like. You?"

"I've uncovered a number of petty thefts, embezzlements, and more illicit affairs than I would have thought possible. I have two minor lackeys reporting to my competition, but no mole. I'm starting to think I don't have one... which means the problem lies entirely with your side, Archer."

That was not what he wanted to hear. "These lackeys. What were they reporting on and to whom?"

"Contract details and income projections. Nothing that would interest the Gray Men."

"Well, at least the gala won't be compromised from your side. That's something." Scott pinched his chin. "Are all the measures in place?"

Royan chimed in. "We've done our best to keep the guests' ships all docked together in a highly secured area. It has easy access to the hotel level where most of them are staying, too. Some have chosen to stay on board their vessels, which works just as well. If anything happens, we can either send them to their ships or the bunker."

"What bunker?" Scott asked.

"Sorry. That's the term we've been using to describe the hotel level the guests are inhabiting. That section of the station has its own water and air supply and can seal itself off to protect the inhabitants," Owen explained, his expression stormy. "It's a unique setup one of the former managers of the station arranged to protect what he deemed were the most important beings on Astek. The rest of the population has no such protection."

"Yet another reason why we need a new, better station. I had no idea about the modifications until Tink found a reference to it." Tianna scowled. "The new station will be a symbol of the changes I'm making to the entire company. This crap *fraxxing* ends. Now. No being on this station is more important than any other."

He knew she meant it. Tianna intended to remake her family's corporation into something far more than it had been under her father's control. She wanted to make a difference, even if it meant she'd become a target for the Gray Men, the shadowy organization made up of corporate leaders, scientists, and influential beings. Their only goals were wealth and power, and they'd happily kill anyone they perceived as a threat to their ambitions.

"Do you have a ready-date for the new station?"

Tianna's lips twitched in a ghost of a smile. "Do you have one for your new station?"

"Is everything a competition with you?" Scott teased.

"Do you have to keep everything a secret?" she replied.

He scowled but answered honestly. "Six months. I'll be making the announcement at the party. The new base is going to be built in situ. A Vardarian company offered to do it. They're expanding operations and thought it would help establish a name for themselves in this sector."

"The IAF is embracing new technology *and* the help of another species?" Tianna placed a dramatic hand over her heart. "What sorcery is this?"

"No magic, just money. They gave us a good deal."

"And it means you're not showing favoritism to any of the shipbuilding companies already here," Tianna said.

"And that. Also, it means that no corporation will be involved in the design or construction. Should reduce the chances we have secret bunkers and spyware built into the damned thing before we even move in."

"That... is an excellent point. I think I might need to hire some of our Vardarian allies to do a thorough inspection before I take possession of the new station."

"Does this station of yours have a name yet?"

"It doesn't. I thought the beings who live there would like to name their home. I just know it won't have my name on it. That's another tradition that died with my father."

"I still think it should have mine. Watson Station. Watson One, Watsonia. You could at least think about it," Royan said.

"No." Both she and Owen spoke together, their tones identical.

It reminded Scott of the way his own trio worked. "I know that tone, Royan. You're not getting your way. They outnumber you."

Royan sighed. "I know." Then he cocked a brow. "Speaking of outnumbering... how are things going with you and Phyl and mister hotter-than-a-supernova-in-a-suit you're spending time with?"

Owen smacked his husband on the shoulder. "You're married."

"I'm married, not dead. And seriously... that man is all kinds of sexy. Even if he is dating my kinda-mom."

"*We* are dating Phyl," Scott clarified.

Royan smirked. "And each other. Right? Because I saw the way he was looking at you and damn..."

"I think this meeting is over," Scott said.

"I think that wasn't a denial." Royan bounced to his feet. "I'm not going to tell you to be good to Phyl. I know you will. I also know if you screw up, she'll deal with you herself. Now, if you'll excuse us, I'd like to head to the Nova Club and collect my winnings."

Scott groaned to himself. "Do I want to know what you were betting on?"

"You really don't," Tianna said. "But I think you can guess."

"You people need a new hobby!" He pointed to the door. "Go. And stop betting on Phylomenia's love life. If she catches you, there will be hell to pay."

Royan laughed. "I wasn't betting on her love life. I was betting on yours."

Owen rolled his eyes. "We're going now, Roy-boy. Time to leave the man who commands a military fleet alone before he decides to make you into a target."

"Tempting," Scott growled as the three filed out. "We'll talk soon."

"Soon," Tianna agreed.

Scott checked the time. He didn't have long before his next meeting. Officially, he was speaking to JAG officer Castille about a couple of cases she was handling. Unofficially, his niece was here to brief him on her investigation into the members of Nova Force Team Three. Time was short, and he had to be sure he could trust them to do what was needed in the coming days. He believed they were clean, but he had to be certain. When the Grays made their move, Nova Force had to be ready to respond. His orders were clear—work with Corp-Sec to protect the station and everyone on it. Nova Force would have to deal with the Grays.

He needed to talk to Bobbi about something else too. He'd arranged for her to be included in the first batch of medi-bot recipients. Now, she had to decide if she wanted the treatment. He'd already made his choice, but he wouldn't tell her he was taking the treatment until she'd decided for herself.

He left the privacy shield up and finished his coffee.

There were too many unknowns and not a lot of time left to find the truth. He snorted and closed his eyes for a moment. "I picked a hell of a time to fall in love again."

Phylomenia sat on a couch near the viewport, her attention shifting between the glorious expanse of stars outside and the spectacular view of Garrett prowling around the suite naked as he took calls and made arrangements for his client and her entourages' arrival.

"I have to admit, I could get used to living like this," she said once he disconnected from yet another audio call. "The view is amazing. The dialogue is a little dry, though."

He grinned. "I feel the same way about flight manifests and cargo logistics, which is why I'm grateful

you've taken a few days off from working. Having you
here with me is the best part of this trip."

Phyl pulled her legs up to make room on the couch.
She was wearing nothing but one of the hotel's plush
robes, which was quite possibly the most comfortable,
cuddly thing she'd ever worn.

Garrett sat down beside her and then drew her legs
across his lap. "What? I know that look, Mena. What
thought is bouncing around your brain that you aren't
keen to say out loud?"

"You shouldn't remember any of my looks. It's
been decades, Gar-Bear."

"It has, but you left a lasting impression. So, what
is it?"

"I was wondering why you didn't move on. You
know. Wife. Husband. Kids. Whatever would have
made you happy."

"It wasn't in the cards for me."

"Explain. Because I don't get it. You're charming,
handsome, have a damned fine ass and no felonies.
What was the problem?"

"My damned fine ass was undercover. My life was
a lie. Anyone I got seriously involved with would be
dragged into that world. I didn't get close enough to
anyone to trust them with the truth, and if I got that
close to someone, I would have never brought them
into that life."

"You're not anymore, though. Right? You could
have settled down with someone by now."

"Not anymore." His answer was as smooth as *keski* silk, but as soon as he spoke, she knew he was lying.

She leaned forward and tapped her finger against his right hand. He'd tucked his thumb inside his fist as he'd spoken. "All this time, and you still haven't fixed your tell."

To her amusement, Garrett actually looked surprised. He glanced down at his hand, undid the fist, and then looked back at her. "I have a tell?"

"You do. And that was it. So, lover of mine. Want to try telling me the truth this time?"

"You've already figured it out. Haven't you?"

"It was a yes or no question. You lied. So yeah, I know the answer. But I want to hear it from you." Because if Garrett was still working for the IAF, that would change things between them all. She didn't know how, exactly, but it would.

"I never resigned my commission. In fact, I've gotten a few promotions. I'm Commander Michaels, Nova Force."

"Nova... wow." She let that sink in for a few seconds before continuing. "Does Scotty know?"

"He does not."

"Who does?" An icy serpent slithered through her guts. Secrets again. That's what had blown their trio up the first time. Were they about to repeat the same mistakes?

"The head of Nova Force. My handler. You. That's it."

"You're a spy."

"A very boring one. Mostly I just do what it says on my business card. I protect pampered corporate executives from angry customers, workers, and each other. If I learn anything of value, I relay it to my handler."

"I don't know if that makes things better or worse. But it does explain why you've never settled down."

"I've had dual loyalties and too many secrets," he admitted. "Plus, there's the whole trust issue. Spend enough time in the waters I swim in and you learn not to trust anyone."

"That's one thing we have in common. Despite the adage, there's not a lot of honor or trust among thieves and smugglers."

He took her hand and squeezed it. "I trust you. That's why this... us." He waved his other hand in the air between them. "It all came back so easily. I haven't had this with anyone since I left you."

"You left us," she said softly and then sighed. "And so did I."

"Ah."

She was in his lap a second later, robe askew, legs bare, his strong arms wrapped around her like twin bars of steel. "You're afraid I'm going to leave again."

"Afraid? I don't do that emotion. I will admit to being... concerned," she said.

"Would it help if I told you I'm thinking of quitting all this? It's not like I need the work."

"You'd do that?"

"I'm tired of secrets. Mostly I'm still doing this because I didn't have anything better to do." He kissed the tip of her nose. "Care to help me find something else to focus on?"

"You could stay here! Or fly with me. And then Archer..." She frowned. "We are including Scott in this. Right? This isn't a you and me plan? It's an all of us together plan. Isn't it?"

"Maybe." The doubt on his face made her heart hurt. "But like you warned me, Scott is married to his work." He gestured around the suite. "Some things haven't changed. The hotel is nicer, but we're still his dirty little secret. He spends his nights with us and then goes back to his other life during the day. I won't live that way. Not again."

"Not again," she agreed. "But if he isn't with us... then what?"

"Then we do this without him. That was my plan the last time I left. Remember? I was coming back for you." His eyes darkened. "But you never made contact. At first I thought you'd stayed with Scott. Later, I tried to find you, but by then you'd paid off your debts and vanished."

"If I'd only known..." Her life would have been so different. But she didn't regret how it had played out. She couldn't. Not when having Garrett meant she would have never met Zura or been part of the family at the Nova Club.

"I know what I want, Mena. Even if Scott makes the same mistake again, I won't."

"I hope it doesn't come to that, but if I have to choose between having neither of you and having only one? Then I know what my choice will be. I've lost too many years with you already. I'm not losing any more."

"Good. Because this time, I'm not letting you go. I still love you, spitfire. I never stopped."

The truth hit her like a comet strike. She'd never stopped loving them, either. Not completely. Now she had nanotech that would keep her alive for centuries. She didn't want to spend them loving someone she couldn't have. They had to make this work. "I love you, too, Garrett. Stars save us all, I do." Then she kissed him before any more of her heart could pour out of her mouth. She'd said enough already.

The chemistry between the two of them was still off the charts. In fact, it was hotter than ever. She half-expected things would settle down after a day or so and the novelty of being back with them would wear off.

It hadn't.

Every touch still made her burn.

Their tongues dueled, mouths mated. She tried to twist in his lap and shed her robe at the same time, but it didn't work quite the way she intended. She managed to pin her own arms to her sides, the fabric trapped under one knee as she straddled his powerful thighs.

"A little help?" she asked, barely breaking the kiss long enough to ask for assistance.

He cupped her shoulders in his hands and then moved them downward until he discovered the problem. The arrogant ass just laughed when he realized what she'd done. She felt a tug at her waist, but instead of freeing her, Garrett used the robe's tie to secure her arms even more firmly at her sides.

"I like you better this way."

"I don't."

He tugged the ends of the tie until the knot was firm and then wrapped both ends in around his fist to pull her in close. "I can change that."

She didn't try to muffle the soft whimper of need that rose from her throat. He knew her too well, and her body had already betrayed her arousal. Her nipples were pebbled as they brushed against the bare skin and hair on his chest. Her cheeks were hot and the folds of her pussy were slick with desire as she ground herself over the thick length of his cock.

"That's right. You take what you need, spitfire."

What she needed was to have him inside her. Now. She didn't want to go slowly. She wasn't interested in a gradual buildup to the main event. He might have tied her hands, but she didn't need them for this.

She leaned into him, rubbing herself cat-like against his hard body as she kissed him and taking control for a moment. His groans vibrated against her lips as the kiss deepened, mouths open, tongues tangled, gasps and soft sounds of desire blending into a kind of sensual music.

Her binding made it impossible for her to do more than touch his torso instead of fist his cock like she wanted to, but she made do. She scratched her nails across his flank and rose as high as she could on her knees, back arched, hips angling as she slid down his body again... and onto his cock.

Garrett uttered her name with an explosive groan as she brought them together, not stopping until he was hilt-deep inside her.

"Naughty." He tried to swat her ass, but his hand hit the fluffy material of her robe and sank into it.

"Fluffy," she corrected him and then nipped his bottom lip. "If you want to spank me, you'll have to untie me. Can't have both."

His eyes darkened. The blue one turning the slate-blue of storm clouds while the green hardened to the color of polished jade. "Are you sure about that?"

She deliberately flexed herself around his cock. "Yup."

He swore in what she was fairly certain was Torski before switching to Galactic Standard. "Wrong."

That's all the warning she got before he released the ends of the belt, took hold of her ass and hips in both hands, and somehow managed to stand while carrying her.

"Hey!" She helped and wrapped her legs around

his hips. It was all she could do since her arms were still bound to her sides. "If you drop me…"

"I will not drop you. I will, however, demonstrate how wrong you are. I can fuck you and spank you without untying you, spitfire. Scotty is going to be sorry he missed this."

"Why don't we call him and see if he wants to come back for a lunchtime quickie?"

Garrett laughed. "Nope. You're not getting out of this so easily. I have plans for you."

She didn't bother to struggle. She knew that whatever he had planned, she'd enjoy it just as much as he did. "Then maybe we should plan for a repeat performance later? Only next time, you tie Scotty up."

His cock swelled and then twitched, giving away his interest.

"Oh, you like that idea. Don't you? You and Scott together, and me watching…"

"Touching yourself," Garrett's voice was little more than a husky whisper as he walked to the end of the couch they'd been sitting on. He kissed her again, hard and hungry, and then lifted her off his cock. She unwound her legs and let him set her back on her feet.

"This doesn't seem so—" she didn't get to finish her sentence before Garrett spun her away from him. A big hand landed between her shoulder blades, pushing her down onto the arm of the couch and holding her there with gentle pressure as he used his feet to prod her legs apart.

He flipped her robe up, exposing her lower body, and then swatted her ass.

"Hey!" she yelped and tried to stand up, but he gently pushed her back down again.

"That's for taking things into your hands."

She wriggled her fingers. "No hands. You tied me up. Remember?"

Smack. Smack. His hand hit just hard enough to sting.

"What the *fraxx* was that for?"

"Sarcasm. Sassing. And because I really like spanking you, Mena mine."

He raised his hand, and she braced for another smack, but instead he caught hold of the ties and drew them upward, coaxing her up onto her toes. "Almost as much as I like do this..."

He aligned their bodies and claimed her in a single thrust that made her gasp and shudder with pleasure.

"Perfection," he murmured.

"Would be if you moved your bossy ass." She tried to move back, but he had her off balance and firmly held by her belt. She couldn't do a thing.

"I missed your fire so much. Missed this." He rocked against her and then withdrew, only to drive into her again. She clenched herself around him, milking his cock as he started to move, slowly at first, but the pace accelerated quickly.

He moved his hands, one taking hold of the belt, the other curving under her to support and balance her as he changed the angle of his thrusts. Now, he was stroking over her g-spot with every thrust.

"Garrett... I can't last if you don't slow down."

"I don't want you to last, sweetheart. I want you to come for me. Scream for me. And I want you to do it *now*."

She could tell by the speed of his strokes he wasn't going to last long, either. She held on to her control just long enough to prove she could and then gave herself over to the pleasure of the moment. She came apart, shattered by a sensual explosion that tore a cry from her lips and made her entire body stiffen and quake.

As she'd hoped, her moment of release pushed Garrett into his. He emptied himself into her with a primal sound she loved.

Spent and panting, Garrett slumped over her, his breath fanning hot against the back of her neck as he freed her from her makeshift bonds.

Phyl didn't move much. She just braced one arm against the side of the couch so she could turn to smile at him over her shoulder. "We are so doing this again tonight. Only next time, I get to watch."

"You figure out a way to convince Scott to let that happen, and I'll make sure we put on a show you never forget." Garrett eased himself away from her a few seconds later, gathered her into his arms and then led her back to the couch to cuddle.

She curled up in his arms, head on his chest, and thought about what he'd said... and what he hadn't.

She wanted to see him with Scott tonight. But she also got the sense they might be doing this to create a memory to hang on to if they couldn't find a way to keep the three of them together.

Scott had to want this. Want them. She just didn't know if he would. At least, not in time to stop them from blowing up again.

10

SCOTT HAD A HUNDRED THINGS HE SHOULD HAVE been doing. The gala kicked off tonight, which meant many of the most powerful people in the galaxy would be gathered in one place, consuming insanely expensive cocktails while indulging in boardroom power games as an even more dangerous game played out around them.

They were bait in a trap, and it was his job to make sure none of them died when the trap slammed shut.

Unfortunately, that was only one of the roles he had to play. He was also one of the guests and would have to take part in the festivities, which meant spending hours making small talk with allies and verbally sparring with the IAF's enemies. He'd enlisted Bobbi's help with both parts of his plan. Her mothers' societal status meant she was at home at events like these, and since she was aware of the true threat, she'd be able to keep an eye on any potential spies in their ranks and let him know when trouble started.

He should have been working, but instead he was walking the main promenade hand in hand with Phylomenia. The odd thing was, he didn't feel guilty about the time away from work.

"You see over there? The way your people are moving as a pack?" Phyl inclined her head toward a group of soldiers. They were off duty, but there was no mistaking who and what they were. From their haircuts to the way they moved, they were clearly military.

"I see them. Calmly and quietly enjoying some time off. What's the problem?"

"Look at the expressions of the beings they pass. The vendors in the promenade are afraid of them."

"Why would—" He stopped talking as he saw what Phyl meant. A tension flowed through the crowd as the soldiers passed. Some stepped back, others dropped their gaze. In the stores, shop owners and even a few customers went still or drifted to a safe spot near the backs of the stores.

"Fraxx."

"Now you see it."

"Wolves among sheep," he said.

"Wolves are extinct. And these beings aren't sheep. They're just ordinary folk trying to survive. And as far as I know, that particular group hasn't caused any trouble."

"You're keeping track?"

"This is my home. I like to know what's happening." Phyl shot him a reproving look. "It's your home, too."

It was on the tip of his tongue to correct her. He didn't have a home. Hadn't had one in years. He had assigned quarters and postings.

He looked around the main concourse. It was familiar. Comfortable. He knew which carts sold his favorite foods and that a shop not far ahead always had his favorite ice cream in stock.

"I hadn't noticed until now, but you're right. It is."

That earned him one of Phyl's special smiles, the kind that lit up her face and made her eyes glow with warmth. "I'm glad to hear that."

He laughed and drew her in for a kiss. "You just like that I said you were right."

Phylomenia blushed.

"What?" he asked, not sure if that was a good sign or a warning signal.

"You kissed me," she whispered. "In public!"

"Well, yeah. I did. You okay with that?"

She actually looked confused for a moment. "Of course I am. Are you?"

"I kissed you. Didn't I? Do I need to kiss you again?" He dropped his mouth to hers and kissed her until she melted against him with a soft moan.

"Keep making noises like that and I will do a lot

more than kiss you the second I get you alone," he warned.

"Now you're just trying to cut short our little tour of the station," she teased. "You asked me to show you what's going on out here in reality. I'd like to show you the rest."

He had asked. Phylomenia had been trying to get him to do this for weeks, and then Bobbi had made the same suggestion while sending him a copy of a report that made it clear there were problems. A Torski girl had been harassed by some off-duty soldiers. Her boyfriend, an IAF private named Reddy, had stepped in. A fight ensued, but the only one arrested had been the boyfriend, with no mention of the others. There was a growing sense of distrust between the military presence and the civilians they were supposed to be protecting.

"Then lead on."

To his surprise, their next stop was only a few steps away. He knew this place. In fact, he'd eaten a meal from here last week. He'd had one of his staff grab it for him, though. He'd been too busy to make the trip out himself, but their *sheka* was delicious, with just the right amount of spice.

"Hello, Atun. How's business today?" Phylomenia greeted the male Pheran working the grill.

"Fair. The usual crowds are all staying away because of the party, and the soldiers are too well-fed to need our wares." He lifted one shoulder. "But we make do. What can I get for you today? Your usual?"

"Two, please." She glanced at Archer. "Actually, better make that three. I'll bring some back for our friend."

Garrett didn't need the meal. He had a fully stocked food dispenser and room service available to him, but the extra scrip would help Atun. He hadn't thought about what would happen to the businesses during the gala. They'd made the decision to limit access to make sure the station wasn't overcrowded. He should have considered what that would do to the ones who relied on that traffic for their livelihoods.

It was too late now. But next time he'd have to do better. Maybe he should try to encourage his people to enjoy the food on offer outside the base. He thought about the way the locals had reacted to the small group of soldiers a moment ago. *Or maybe not.*

"Scott, I'd like to introduce you to Atun and Ma'ti."

"We haven't been introduced, but I am very fond of your *sheka*. Scott Archer. Nice to meet you, Atun." He turned and nodded to Ma'ti. "And you as well. Your toral loaf is some of the best I've ever had."

Phylomenia looked surprised and then grinned. "Nice to know you do get out of your office sometimes."

"Sometimes," he admitted. "Though usually I have someone pick me up an order."

That made the Pheran male's ears twitch and some

of the warmth left his expression, though his smile didn't change. "Ah, now I remember. You are not just Scott Archer. You are *Colonel* Archer."

"I am. But not right now. At the moment, I'm just Scott."

Atun's ears twitched again. "As you say."

"I wanted you to meet these two for a reason." Phyl squeezed his hand. "Members of the Pheran delegation are causing problems. They've been harassing some of the citizens of this station, including Atun and Ma'ti. The delegates believe they can do it because they are *Taryn-nah*, the elite class."

"That system has been outlawed by their own government."

"Yet they're still taking food and goods without paying for it because they think it is their right."

"Phyl! We do not need to bother the colonel about such things," Ma'ti hissed, her stripes darkening as she shot a worried glance at Scott.

"He needs to know." Phyl glanced over at him. "Don't you?"

"I do." He'd seen a report referencing the problem, but he'd set it aside because he had more pressing concerns. Station security was Astek and Corp-Sec's problem. At least, that's what he'd told himself at the time.

"If anyone else gives you trouble, contact me." He tapped his comms and sent a contact link to the comm unit sitting beside the grill. Then he quickly sent a payment to the vendor's machine to cover lunch before Phylomenia could. "That is a direct line. You won't have to talk to anyone but me."

"And if you see any of the IAF making trouble, you let one of us know. Okay?" Phylomenia added. "I'm staying on the station for a bit. I'll come by anytime." She grinned. "And I have a couple of cyborgs I'm happy to bring along for backup."

Both Pherans relaxed enough to laugh, and Ma'ti gave him a shy smile. "You will help us? Really?"

"I will. That's part of our mission."

Phyl made a soft, approving sound and went to pay.

Atun waved her off. "It's already taken care of. He paid while you talked."

"You did? Who are you and what did you do with the real Archer?"

He kissed the tip of her nose. "I already told you. Today, I'm just Scott."

"Well, just Scott. I hope Archer doesn't come back anytime soon. I like this version better."

"He'll be back tonight, but I'll see if I can ditch him before I get back to you and Garrett."

They made their way to an empty table and spread their meal out between them.

"You mean that. Don't you?" Phyl asked, her voice soft.

"Which part?"

"Ditching Archer before you come back to us."

Us. Her and Garrett. There'd been a time he hadn't liked hearing her using words like that. It made him feel like an outsider.

Not this time.

"I do. I'll be home late, but I will be there."

"Good. I'll be waiting for both of you." She smiled and bit into her *sheka*.

He took a moment to rub the side of his neck. He'd had his injection of medi-bots a few hours ago. It was one more thing he and Phyl had in common now, and it made him want to include her in more of his life—even the parts she hadn't been too fond of the last time. "Would you like to come as my date tomorrow night? To the gala, I mean."

"You're asking me to get dressed up and make small talk like a good little military spouse already?" she asked, one brow arched and her expression suddenly wary.

"No. I'm asking the woman I love to come with me to a fancy party with excellent food so I have someone to talk to who won't bore me to tears."

She dropped her food, bounced out of her chair and landed on his lap two steps later. "That's it. Archer is never allowed to come back. Ever!"

He wrapped his arms around her, amused at her antics and pleased to see her so happy. "Because I said I love you?"

"Because Archer never could. Not in public. Not

once." She kissed him gleefully, making enough fuss that several other patrons stared. He ignored them.

"That man was clearly an idiot. I do love you, and I'm fine with letting the universe know about it."

"Miracles abound," she declared, stealing one of Garrett's more annoying phrases.

"What would be miraculous was if you actually answered my question. Will you be my date tomorrow night?" He hadn't had to work this hard to get a yes in years.

He gazed into Phylomenia's eyes and saw something new. Hope. For them. For this.

For us.

"Yes. Oh, and in case I forgot to mention it? I love you, too."

"Excellent. I've been told there will be an ice cream station. We'll have to see if we can replicate that beast of a dessert from the Brass Tactics."

Phyl patted her stomach and managed a seductive little wiggle at the same time. "You're on. Last time I didn't have a nanotech-enhanced metabolism. I will eat you both under the table."

"Care to make a bet on that?" he asked, reaching past her to pick up her forgotten *sheka* and placing the spicy meat-filled loaf back in her hands. "This is ice cream we're talking about. I think I'm up for the challenge."

"What are the stakes?" Instead of eating her meal,

she broke off a piece and fed it to him, delaying his answer a few seconds.

"I think we should let Garrett decide," he said, well aware of the risk he was taking. Over the last few days their lover had revealed he'd developed some intriguing new interests and a fertile imagination.

She took another bite before declaring, "I don't know if that means you think you'll win, or if you're hoping to lose."

"This bet involves ice cream and nudity. I'm seeing this as a more of a win-win."

"You have an excellent point there, sir."

"I thought so, too. Feel like doing a practice run this afternoon?"

"Practice run?" she asked, eyes glinting.

"Mmhm. You. Me. Chocolate sundaes. Plan A is we eat them at this little place I know."

"What's Plan B?" she asked, already rising from his lap.

"We order it to go, and then we both get sticky."

"Oh, I like Plan B. Your treat, my ship?"

"Perfect."

"Then let's go." She tossed him his still-wrapped *sheka*. "You can eat that on the way. You're going to need your strength."

"Why am I surrounded by bossy people these days?" he grumbled as he got to his feet.

"You're blessed. That's why. Now, which way is this ice cream you promised me?"

He took her hand and led her down the concourse. Work could wait a little longer. He had better things to do.

Garrett enjoyed most aspects of his job. However, prowling parties full of self-important idiots all trying to impress other idiots was not one of them.

He'd seen so much posturing, bravado, and bullshit tonight he was dying to dull some of the pain with champagne, but since he was working, he had to settle for a sparkling fruit juice instead.

At least he didn't need to stick close to his client. She had her own security for that. Terra Fox was the new CEO of Bellex Shipbuilding, and she was smart enough to trust him to do his job without interference.

He'd met with her on her ship and briefed her on his findings and recommendations before she'd even set foot on Astek Station.

To her credit, she'd listened to him—something far too few of his clients did, especially considering how much they paid for his advice. At some events he felt more ornamental than useful. Thankfully, that wasn't the case this time.

Terra Fox caught his eye, and he gave her a casual nod. *All quiet. Nothing to report.*

She raised a glass to her lips, hiding her subtle nod

behind it before moving on. One more shark swimming through the dark waters, looking for her next victim.

He went back to work, watching for signs of trouble… or the Gray Men. They'd be here, somewhere. He'd done this job too long not to know about the mysterious group who made so much of the galaxy dance to their tune. He just didn't know who any of them were.

Scott hadn't said anything. He couldn't. But Garrett had been at this a long time and he knew a trap when he walked into one. Astek might be looking for a way to bring everyone together and stop another expensive war, but that wasn't the only reason they were all here.

They were bait.

Scott was holding court in another part of the elaborately decorated ballroom. He wasn't the highest-ranking officer in the room, but he was the one everyone wanted to speak to. Garrett felt a stir of pride. Scott really had done well for himself.

The entire area reeked of wealth and privilege with thick burgundy carpets that absorbed most of the noise and polished furniture of real wood imported in from some distant planet. Servers offered appetizers of rare and expensive food and elegant crystal glasses with liquors from all over the galaxy.

The other high-ranking IAF officer present was Brigadier General Halverson, a pompous pain in the ass Garrett had crossed paths with before. He was a fixture at events like these, basking in the trappings of power. He was the opposite of Scotty in every way. A loud, arrogant, braggart who had a habit of fouling up any operation he decided to stick his pudgy nose into. The last he'd heard, the man was supposed to be banned from this part of space. How the *fraxx* he'd scored an invitation to the party was anyone's guess. When he'd asked Scott about it, all he'd gotten was a pained look and a heavy sigh.

Scott didn't like the man, either.

Halverson worked the room, his aide never more than a few steps from his side. Scott had a different approach. He stayed still and let others come to him. He also had a pretty JAG officer with obvious experience at these events acting as his go-between, making contact and bringing over anyone Scott wanted to speak with.

The JAG officer looked oddly familiar, but only when she came close did he realize why. She had Scott's eyes.

Did Scott have a daughter? That didn't seem likely. He called up his list of attendees and scrolled through it, looking for her photo. Lieutenant Commander Castille. Ah. That explained it. Not his daughter, his niece.

One he hadn't mentioned was on the station.

Garrett's jaw clenched. Secrets. Again.

He let the security team with his client know he was taking a break and left the bustle of the main hall.

The lobby had stations for drinks and appetizers, and an opportunity for small groups to gather in relative quiet. He refreshed his drink and then found a peaceful corner, enjoying the cooler air and elegant patterns of the lights swirling and dancing near the lobby ceiling. It helped, but it wasn't enough. He needed to talk to the one person who could unruffle his feathers. Mena.

She answered his vid-call quickly, smiling up at him from the screen of his comms. "Hey, handsome, having fun?"

"Not really. What are you up to?"

"Quality time with the sprites." She moved her comm so he could see the silver-eyed baby with chubby cheeks and a heart-melting smile seated in her lap. "This is Mya."

"Where's Dana?"

"Currently trying to pull my shoe off," Phylomenia said with a laugh.

"I wish I could be there to help her." Hearing her laugh was a balm to his turbulent mood.

"What's wrong?"

"Archer."

"Back to being on a last name basis? What did he do now?"

"Did you know he's got family on the station?"

"No! Who?"

Her surprise made it easier to breathe. It was obvious this time she hadn't been in on the secret.

"Lieutenant Commander Roberta Castille. Unless I'm mistaken, she's got to be Celeste's little girl. She married into that family. And the Lieutenant Commander is JAG."

"*Fraxxing* hell. Celeste's kid is old enough to be a lawyer?"

"Afraid so. And she's here on Astek, apparently working with Scott."

"That man has more secrets than underwear. Does she know you know? Does he?"

"Don't think so. I didn't make the connection until I saw her up close. She has her mother's eyes, and they're the same as her uncle's." He'd met Scott's sister a handful of times at events like this one. Her wife was a judge on the Unified Galactic Supreme Court and came from an influential family.

"You think he's keeping secrets again." It wasn't a question.

"I know he is. He's not even looked my way tonight, either. I might as well be invisible."

"Gar-Bear, stop. You're working. He's working. Tonight is not the time to start making judgments. Wait until tomorrow night."

"That's not going to be any better. We'll still be working."

"I'll be there tomorrow. Scott asked me to come as his date, and now I'm asking you." She winked. "Wanna go to a party with me?"

"You're coming here? To the gala?" He tried and

failed to keep the anger out of his voice. This event was the one place in the galaxy he did *not* want her to be. Especially not tomorrow night, which was the pinnacle of the event and would be standing room only.

"I am. Why? Don't you want me there?"

Fraxx. Now he'd hurt her feelings when the one he wanted to hurt was Scott. In the face. Repeatedly.

He and Scott had to be in attendance. This was what they got paid to do, but for the love of gravity. Why would Scott invite the woman they cared for to ground-zero for whatever the Gray Men had planned?

"I do. Always. But not tomorrow night. There are things you don't know about, Mena. He's doing it again. Keeping secrets and putting the ones he cares about in the line of fire." He scrubbed a hand over his beard. "This stops. Now."

"Don't do anything—"

He ended the call, dropped his comm unit into his pocket, and marched back into the main hall. He needed a word with Scott, and he was going to get one. *Now.*

Scott was still parked where he'd been most of the evening, which made him easy to find. Garrett cut through the crowd like a plasma torch, not stopping until he reached his objective. Scott was momentarily alone. Even the dour Nova Force officer who had been acting as his personal bodyguard was nowhere to be seen.

"We need to talk."

Scott frowned. "Trouble? Where? Is Phyl alright?"

"Yes. Here. And she's what we need to talk about." It took him a moment to locate an empty alcove. It was some distance away, but what he needed to say had to be done in private, and the conversation alcoves were all fitted with sound dampeners for exactly that purpose. "That one. Move."

Scott shot him a look of pure annoyance. "Don't take that tone with me in public."

"Why not? It's the only way I can get you to pay attention to me when we're *in* public."

He stalked off, not giving Scott a chance to respond. He briefly wondered if his lover would follow him and was gratified when Scott appeared at his shoulder a few steps later.

"So, we're at that stage of the relationship already?"

"Which stage?"

"Drama. Fighting. I figured we had a few more days."

"Asshole."

"Me? I'm not the one creating a scene right now."

They entered the nook and immediately the background hum of conversation dropped to a whisper.

"So, what's this about? What's wrong with Phyl?" Scott asked.

"You are. You could have talked to me before asking her to this event. Instead, I find out hours later, and only because Phylomenia told me about it."

"I was going to tell you later tonight. Why are you so pissed off? I thought you'd be happy," Scott said.

"That you're bringing the woman we adore to the most dangerous place on the *fraxxing* station?"

"Because I want her close at hand so *we* can protect her."

"She's safer at the Nova Club. Or at my hotel," Garrett snarled and stepped in closer.

"Is that what you think? I thought you were a security expert!" Scott snapped back.

"I am. Which is why I know this whole party is bait for a trap for the Grays. Or did you think no one else would figure that out? You invited our spitfire to be your date at arma-*fraxxing*-geddon. Does she know what's happening, or did you leave her in the dark the same way you did Tim?"

Scott's eyes darkened and his expression held all the threat of an oncoming storm. "Don't. That's not what's happening here."

"Then tell me what is because so far all I know is you're keeping secrets again. Mena. The fact that Celeste's daughter is here..."

"You're not supposed to know that!"

"Please. I've met the girl's mothers more than once. And she has your eyes. It wasn't hard to figure out."

"You can't know that. No one can know that. It wouldn't be safe for her..."

"So you're not just putting Phylomenia in danger but your own niece, too? *Fraxxing* hell, Scott. When will you stop putting duty over everything and everyone?" Garrett was certain now. History was repeating itself, only this time, Garrett saw it coming. If Scott wanted to go down this path, he'd do it alone. He and Phylomenia would take another path... together.

"That's not what's happening!"

They were interrupted by the momentarily absent Nova Force officer who barely managed to snap off a salute before asking, "Everything alright here, sir?"

"Fine," Scott barked.

"Of course you'd think that," Garrett muttered and stormed out, deliberately shouldering Scott out of his way. It was the closest he could get to punching him... for now. This conversation wasn't over, though. Later tonight the three of them needed to have this out, and if Scott didn't change his ways, he'd be out, too.

11

Phylomenia didn't say much as Garrett paced in relentless circles while they waited for Scott to arrive.

They were back at the hotel, and Garrett was fit to be tied. In fact, she was tempted to tie him to a chair to stop him from going after Scott the second he walked through the door.

"If you growl one more time, I swear I'm going to find a stunner and drop you where you stand," she said as he prowled past her for what seemed like the hundredth time.

"I'm not..." He stopped and cleared his throat. "Okay, I am. But dammit, where is he?"

"Dealing with the evening's fallout. You had one client to take care of. He's responsible for all of them."

"Why are you taking his side?" he demanded.

"Why are you being this crazy?" she asked.

"Because he's putting you at risk!"

So that's what this was about. "You've been as grumpy as a Torski with a sore tooth because you think Scott put me in danger?"

"Yes!"

She pointed to an empty chair. "Sit."

"I'd rather stand."

"Sit!"

He dropped into the chair. "Happy now?"

"Not really. It's very sweet that you're all worked up because you think I need protecting from Scott's plans."

"You don't know—"

"That it's a trap to lure the Grays into taking a shot at us?" she finished for him. "Do you really think I didn't know? You and Scotty really don't think I'm all that bright. Do you?"

"That's not it. We just..." Garrett shrugged. "So, he told you?"

Phyl scoffed. "He didn't have to. Zura and her family are survivors. So am I. We see what's happening. Even if we hadn't, Tianna's husband is Zura's brother. Did you really think he wouldn't have warned her? Hell, he and her husbands tried to get her to leave the station before this all kicked off. She's as stubborn as her father and was having none of it."

"The only ones who don't have a clue are the bait in this trap and the civilians who have no idea this whole station is a target. Even some of them decided it was a good time to head out to visit family or take that long-delayed holiday anywhere but here."

"So, you knew, and you didn't tell me." She heard the bitterness in his voice.

"It's not like that, Gar-Bear. I assumed that as a seriously talented security officer, you'd already worked that out on your own. I mean, it's obvious. Even the Grays must know it's a trap. It's just so tempting they're likely to try anyway. I wasn't keeping secrets. I thought you knew."

"I did. I didn't realize you did..." He trailed off.

"So you didn't tell me, and I didn't tell you. We still suck at communication, lover."

His stance softened and the lines around his eyes deepened as he smiled a little. "We do. Going to have to work on that.

"Yeah." She sat back. "But I'm starting to think that you and Archer aren't as smart as I gave you credit for. You both seem to think the gala is going to be the main target."

"Of course it is. Every corporation in the galaxy sent representatives to this thing."

"Yup," she drawled. "And I'm sure they're hoping to send a message to the corporations about the dangers of standing up to them. But that's not the only target on this station." She'd worked this out weeks ago. They all had. Well, everyone at the Nova Club, anyway. "My family is on their kill list, Garrett. The Gray Men want them dead."

She saw the moment the lights went on. "You lot have been making plans for this. Haven't you?"

"We have. If the shit hits the fan, the Nova Club will be the safest place on the station, bar none. If they attack the club, we'll have time to evac. If they go after our ships? We'll stay at the club. We're ready. Did you really think I would leave any of this to chance?"

Garrett's mouth opened and closed a few times before he finally answered. "Does Scotty know?"

It was the first time he'd used the more familiar version of Scott's name since he'd stormed through the door.

"He's got enough on his plate already." She shrugged. "And he knows I can take care of myself."

"You shouldn't have to. You have us to—"

She cut him off. "Nope. That ship is not going to fly. Put the SS *Damsel in Distress* back in her docking bay, Garrett. I don't need rescuing. I never did. What I wanted was to know that the men in my life would be there for me when I needed them."

He had the grace to look abashed. "Yeah. I *fraxxed* that up."

"We all did. You. Me. Scotty. I wasn't there for you, either. This isn't about blame." She waved a hand.

"We are light years past that now. But we need to do better this time."

"We do." He scrubbed a hand over his beard. "Which means I need to apologize to Scott for nearly decking him at the party tonight... Doesn't it?"

She laughed. "It might be a good place to start. Especially since the plan was never to exclude you... I asked him not to tell you so I could ask you myself."

"*Fraxx.* You did?"

"I did. Which is what I was trying to tell you when you disconnected our call." She was tempted to add "idiot" to the end of the sentence but decided it was already implied. Especially since she had a share of the blame. Secrets had torn them apart before. She should have been smarter.

This was why she avoided serious relationships. They were harder to navigate than a debris field while traveling at full thrust.

As if to underscore her thoughts, Scott pinged her comms at that moment.

It was a single line of text. *"Safe to approach?"*

"Scott wants to know if he can come in. Can he?" she asked Garrett.

Garrett grunted. "Yeah."

"Good." She sent Scott an all clear and waited to see how long it took for him to appear.

Ten seconds later, he walked through the door. He hadn't even changed out of his uniform yet, though the collar was loosened. His hands were fisted at his sides, his lips pressed thin.

"What happened?" Phyl rose and went over to him, slipping her arms around his waist and giving him a hug.

"He didn't tell you?" Scott asked.

"Some of it. You two fought. There was some kind of blowup between your people and the Pherans, and the locals are banding together to protest the current state of affairs on this station. None of that's good, but it doesn't explain why you look like you went to war instead of a party."

"Two of my officers got involved in a fracas with the Pheran trade ambassador. He attacked a Pheran server who was pushed into him. Castille stepped in to protect the server and the *fraxxing* asshole clawed her. Then Meyer got involved."

"Kurt? Nova Force?"

"That's the one. I think he's got a thing for..." Scott grunted. "She's my niece. Roberta Castille. I'm sure he told you that already, but I wanted you to hear it from me. You can't tell anyone, though. That would just put her in more danger than she's already in."

She glanced at Garrett, who shrugged and gave her a "I told you so" look.

Celeste's daughter was really here on Astek. Working for Scott. More secrets. Wonderful. Though she understood the reason why he'd keep this one.

"I think the three of us need to sit down and talk."

"I can do that." Scott bowed his head to kiss her cheek. "I missed you."

Garrett got to his feet and Scott tensed again, shifting their positions so he was between her and Garrett.

"Relax. I'm joining you to apologize. And because I'd like in on the hugging action you two have going on." Garrett wrapped them both in his arms and sighed. "This is better."

Then he turned to Scott. "I'm sorry about earlier. Secrets... they're an issue for me. But I didn't give you or Mena a chance to explain before I went off."

"At least you didn't tackle me this time. So, we're making progress?" Scott laughed and leaned in to kiss Garrett's cheek. "Asshole."

"Idiot. I thought you were putting our spitfire in the line of fire."

"I know. And I know why you thought that. But that's not the plan. I want her with us so we can protect her."

"Again with the protection thing," Phylomenia grumbled. "You two do remember that *I'm* the criminal in this relationship? If anything, I should be protecting the two of you."

"Noted. Still not going to happen but noted," Scott said, and then he kissed her properly—hot, hungry, and possessive.

"You know... you do have a point, Mena mine. Not about you being the criminal... I'm glossing over that bit for my mental well-being. You do, however, have nanotech we do not. So... feel free to protect me from anything that you can heal from and I can't."

"Did you just ask our woman to take a proverbial bullet for you?" Scott asked, slightly horrified.

"I'm just saying only one of us is mostly bulletproof. Upon further consideration of that fact, I'm good with being protected. For now." He glowered at her. "The second I figure out how to get a dose of that for myself? You're back to being the protectee."

"Sure thing, Gar-Bear. All the protecting. You need to let go of us to pound your chest for a bit or are you good?" It was easy to tease them now that things were back on track again. In fact, it was better this way.

"That's enough sass out of you, missy. Come on. I think Scotty needs a shower. We should help him with that. Then we can talk about things, including the plan for tomorrow night."

Scott groaned and nodded. "Shower. Yes, please. I cannot wait to get out of this uniform."

She'd never thought she'd hear him say that. Maybe Scott wasn't completely married to his work after all.

"Just so you know. I still can't tell you everything, but I'll share everything I can. Okay?" Scott said as they led him to the sanitation room.

"Fair enough."

Garrett's acceptance came so quickly it gave Phylomenia pause. Was there something he hadn't told them? If they survived the next few days, they'd have to address that issue eventually, but not tonight.

They'd just survived their first fight. That was something to celebrate.

12

Having Phylomenia at his side made the second night of the gala far more pleasurable for Scott. He had someone to talk to besides the other guests, and her presence helped to settle him in ways Scott hadn't expected. Just knowing she was nearby improved his mood. So did seeing more of Garrett. He came to speak to Phylomenia several times, bringing her tidbits and drinks and making sure she was taken care of when Scott was caught up in the business of the night.

They both looked incredible. Garrett was in a tailored suit that shimmered with a hint of blue-green light, bringing out the color of both his eyes. Phylomenia was stunning in an evening gown of deep blue and crimson, the rough-and-ready pilot almost invisible beneath the veneer of polish and elegance she wore like a personal shield.

This is what he'd envisioned for them back in the day. At least, the part about having Phylomenia with him. He'd always told himself that nothing had happened with Garrett because Garrett wasn't ready for it. The truth was, neither of them had been ready. Back then he'd been focused on his ambitions, on getting ahead and making no waves that might knock him off course.

Standing here tonight, he questioned what the hell his younger self was thinking. Ambition was a fine thing to have... in theory. But in reality, he'd let his family's expectations push him to put his career ahead of everything else, including himself. If he could go back in time, he'd do things differently. Then maybe he wouldn't have lost all that time with Phylomenia and Garrett, and Phaedra would have grown up knowing more about her father than a couple of old holo-pics and her mother's memories.

The need to do things differently was why he'd changed tactics and ensured that Bobbi wasn't in attendance tonight. He'd used her very public confrontation with the Pheran as an excuse to remove her from his list of invitees. It would keep her away from ground zero tonight, and out of Brigadier General Halverson's sight. The man was pompous and dangerously ignorant, but he did have influence, and right now he was using all of it to try and derail Scott's career. He didn't want Bobbi caught in the backlash.

At least, that had been the plan. He'd forgotten to consider the fact Bobbi was as stubborn as her mothers.

She'd come anyway, dressed to kill and flaunting an invitation from Tianna Astor herself.

"If you glare any harder at that girl, people are going to notice. The point of keeping her away from here was to make her less of a target, right? So stop making it so obvious she's someone you care about." Phylomenia took his hand and then leaned into his side. "She knows what she's doing. Stop worrying."

"Says the woman who was lecturing me not that long ago about the fact I still keep putting the people I care about in danger."

"Well, you do. But not this time. She came here knowing the risks." Phyl lowered her voice. "And so did I."

"If it goes badly, I want you to go with Garrett."

"I'd rather stay with you both."

"I'd rather that, too. But you and I are both targets. Having us in the same place isn't smart. Besides, Garrett doesn't have medi-bots. You do."

"So after all your teasing last night, now you're asking me to protect him?"

"I want both my lovers back in my arms when this is over, so yes. I'm asking. Because as much as it pains me to admit it, he was right. You're not the one who needs our protection."

"And if I'm keeping Garrett alive, whose taking care of you?"

"You are no longer the only nanotech enhanced badass in our trio." He'd just broken enough orders and top-secret classifications to get him court martialed three times over, but this was too important. She needed to know.

Her eyes widened. "When?"

"Yesterday. And before you say anything, I know, I should have told you both last night." He'd planned on it. But by the time they'd showered, talked through some things, and made love to each other, all three of them had been ready to call it a night.

She snorted and patted his arm. "It's fine. You and Garrett are both out of practice at telling the truth. I've clearly got a thing for men who lie for a living. I should probably book some time with Dr. Virness to discuss it."

"Nope. Your taste in men is perfect. Don't you dare change a thing."

She laughed and kissed his cheek. "You would say that."

He was about to say something flirtatious when he caught sight of Bobbi dancing with Kurt. The chemistry between them was tangible. "I knew it."

"Knew what?"

"Meyer and Bobbi." He nodded toward the dance floor.

"Oh, I see," Phyl grinned. "I thought he was going to melt into the floor when she walked in tonight. Now I see why. He's smitten."

"With *my* niece."

"A fact that poor boy is not aware of. If he were, he'd probably have saluted and asked permission before even looking at her. Now, stop glowering. If she's with him, she's got a protector for the night. Though honestly, I'm starting to wonder if the Grays are going to try anything. Maybe they decided it was too obvious?"

"Maybe. But let's not tempt the universe by saying anything more."

He was still watching as the dance ended and Meyer led Bobbi off the floor. He was about to turn away when the two kissed.

"If you don't stop growling, I'm going to get jealous, Scotty."

"She's my sister's kid. Closest thing I have to a daughter..."

"I know. And I love that you're all growly and protective of her. It's adorable."

"You're trying to distract me by insulting me now?"

She didn't deny it. "Is it working?"

"Yes." He winked at her. "Now I would like to reward you. Care to dance with me, Captain Harrington?"

"I would be honored, Colonel Archer."

The dance floor was another pretense—a raised dais that had appeared suddenly, rolling out of a hidden space behind one wall. The blue and silver floor pulsed and swirled in time to the music with railings to keep the dancers safely away from the edge. It wasn't large, but not enough beings were using it to make it overly crowded. Besides, the music was good and it gave him a chance to hold Phylomenia close.

Part way through the song, Garrett joined them. "May I cut in?"

"Yes," Phylomenia said.

"No," Scott said at the same moment.

"No?" Garrett's eyes darkened instantly.

It was time to show Garrett that things really were different this time. "Cool your boosters, idiot. I want you to join us."

"I think that's my move," Phylomenia said. Her eyes were bright with approval and joy as she moved back to give Garrett space to add himself.

"I'm borrowing it," Scott said.

Garrett stepped into the gap. It meant he had Phylomenia on one side and Garrett on the other, all of them with their hands on each other's backs and fingers interlocked.

It felt right. In fact, it felt perfect.

Phylomenia could have spent the rest of the night on that dance floor. Not that she was much of a dancer, but something had been magical about the three of them holding on to each other. It was a very public announcement. One she couldn't have imagined happening the last time they were together.

Not even the judgmental glare of the obnoxious General Halverson could affect her buoyant mood as they descended the stairs and returned to the reality of the evening.

Garrett slipped away to check on his client while she and Archer returned to their previous position. Barely more than a minute had passed before Nyx, Nova Force's first cyborg member, appeared and headed straight for them.

When a former assassin looked as serious as Nyx did at the moment, it wasn't a good sign.

"Excuse me a moment. Will you?" Scott said. A moment later, he and Nyx were deep in conversation.

When he returned to Phyl, she braced for bad news. "What happened?"

"It's starting. We need to find Garrett."

It was a matter of moments to track down the big man and then make their way over to him, and another few seconds to find an empty alcove where they could talk in peace.

"Trouble?" Garrett asked.

"They're here. Now. There's been a handoff between an IAF member and Halverson's man, Clooney. No idea what was transferred, but if they need to get away, we have to assume there's a diversion planned."

"How much of this am I supposed to know?" Garrett asked.

"None of it. But get your client out of here anyway. You can tell her Tianna's speech tonight is about Astek building a new station out here. Then I was going to announce the same thing for the IAF. A permanent base of operations in the Drift."

Garrett's lips thinned. "How bad is it going to get?"

"I want you to take our spitfire with you. I have to stay here. You two don't. Bobbi's gone. Not sure where yet, but I'm working on it. Take care of each other and get somewhere safe."

"Watch your ass, Scotty. I want you back in one piece, too." Phylomenia threw herself into his arms and kissed him, her stomach dropping as a premonition of loss hit her. If this was the last time they were together...

"I'll take care of our spitfire. You take care of yourself. When this is over, ice cream sundaes and Star Blood shots. You hear me?" Garrett wrapped Scott in a bear hug. "Don't you die on us now."

"Not on the agenda. Too much else to do." Scott slapped Garrett on the ass. "Now let go and get out of here. We've got work to do."

They let go of each other, and another wave of dread washed over her. "I love you both so much. Thank you for this last week. It's been..."

Garrett stopped her with a kiss. "It's not over, Mena mine. Don't you dare start talking that way."

"Go. Stay alive. Now I'm leaving before this gets any more emotional." Scott smiled and then turned, walking back into the party and away from them.

She let herself feel the weight of the moment for another heartbeat and then locked it all away. "Okay. So, where's your client?"

"This way. Her name's Terra Fox. Play nice." He took her by the hand, leading her toward an elegantly dressed woman standing not far away.

"Hello, Garrett. Enjoying yourself?" Terra asked before he could say a word. While she spoke to him, her eyes never left Phylomenia.

"He is," Phyl declared, letting her claws show a little. "Aren't you, Gar-Bear?"

"I was. Amazing party. But I'm afraid I need to step out for a bit. Family emergency."

To her credit, Terra didn't bat an eyelid. "I see. Back home or somewhere nearby?"

"Home."

This time, Terra's mask cracked. It was only for a second, but it was enough for Phylomenia to spot the other woman's fear. Then Terra composed herself and her next words came out coated in ice.

"So, you're breaking your contract and leaving early? Wonderful. Since I am about to be abandoned to my own devices, I think I'll retire early."

"My apologies. I'll send you a modified bill shortly along with a report detailing what happened."

"That... would be appreciated." Terra dismissed them with a nod.

They hadn't made it more than a few steps before Terra had vanished, whisked away by her security force.

"That was smooth," Phyl said. "But I still don't like her. She thought your *personal* services were part of the contract. Didn't she?"

Garrett choked, but when he looked at her, his cheeks were red. "She might have misunderstood the agreement initially, but I clarified things for her."

"If she *misunderstands* again, I'll do more than clarify things."

"No airlocks. I'm off the market. And even when I wasn't... she is not my type."

"Good answer." She had a brief pang of regret as they passed the dessert tables that had just been set up. She hadn't even gotten to stay for dessert.

"Later. All you can eat." He said as he pulled her along.

"I wasn't going to stop. I do have some common sense, you know."

He chuckled but didn't say another word until they were in the lobby and out of earshot of the other guests.

"I know. But for once, I think we should do exactly as Scott said. So, where's the safest place on the station?"

"The Nova Club or your hotel level. But my family is at the Nova."

"Then that's where we're going. Bullet train?"

"Fastest way I can think of," she agreed.

The second they walked through Astek's front doors, she knew that wasn't going to be an option. Angry crowds filled the area, some of them holding signs and others chanting slogans. There was no way through, especially not for two people dressed in evening wear. Anyone who saw them would know where they'd been.

Garrett huffed in frustration. "*Fraxx*. New plan."

"Is this the one that starts with 'get anywhere that isn't here'?"

"That's the one. Thoughts?"

"Back inside. I need to get a second opinion." She pulled him back through the doors as the crowd spotted them and surged forward.

"Anyone who leaves that way risks getting torn apart by that crowd," Garrett said.

"Which is probably why they've been lured here." Phyl took a few steps into the lobby and raised her voice. "Tink. You around, sweetheart? I need a word."

A shimmering ball of light streaked down from the ceiling and coalesced into a hologram of a winged fairy. "Hello, Phylomenia. What can I do for you?"

"Tell Tianna and her boys they've got an angry mob out front for one thing, and then tell me another way out of here. I need to get to the Nova Club."

"Message sent. I recommend departing through those doors. They will take you to another exit near the commercial docking rings. You should be clear to make your way back to the club from there."

"Thank you."

"Of course." Tink vanished in a puff of glitter.

"We're getting intel from fairies now?" Garrett looked dubiously at the sparkling cloud of glitter that vanished as it hit the floor.

"From one fairy, yes. That's Tink, Tianna Astor's personal AI. That program probably knows more about what's going on inside these walls than we do."

"I thought AIs weren't allowed to be that uh..." he frowned.

"Aware? Human? Yeah... she's on the bleeding edge of legal. Fortunately, she's on our side."

They lapsed into silence for the next while, both of them focusing their awareness on their surroundings as they navigated the unfamiliar corridors.

"Are you armed?" Garrett's question came out of the blue and seemed too loud in the empty hall.

"Do you really need to ask that?" She stopped to look at him, her voice low.

He winked at her. "I wanted to be sure. Later, you can show me where you're hiding it."

"Later," she agreed, trying to ignore the whispers at the back of her mind that said there wouldn't be a later. Not for them.

"Comms?" he asked.

"Purse." She touched the small bag that had been

slung over her shoulder all night. It was the only reason she had the damned thing.

He frowned. "Are you carrying the same clunky beast you've owned since the first time we met?"

"Clunky outer shell only. Inside is state of the art. It deters thieves."

"Dammit. I should have thought of this before now. I really do need to think about retiring. If things go nova, standard comms will probably go down."

He pulled several wafer-thin objects from his pocket and handed one to her.

"If we get separated, use this to contact me. It's a hardened network that only links to my comm."

"You carry these around with you? Is this how you used to pick up dates?"

"I'm not answering that right now. Just use it if you need to."

She slipped the card-sized comm unit into her gown's only pocket, a tiny pouch on one hip she had dismissed as useless given the way the dress fit, but the card was thin enough to slide in without showing.

They set off again, reaching the door to the docking ring after what felt like an endless walk through the service tunnels. At least the way was well-marked.

The exit was a pair of double doors that swung on old-fashioned hinges instead of hydraulics. She checked them. Sure enough, the hinges were a new addition. Instead of replacing the more expensive system, someone had just bolted cheap hinges to the wall and hung the doors on them.

"Shoddy," Garrett murmured.

"And cheap," she agreed.

Garrett cracked the door open and checked what lay beyond. Voices carried through the opening, and both of them froze.

"Why isn't he underway already?" a woman demanded, her tone frosty and frustrated.

"He's being cautious. He knows what's at stake," a male replied.

"But the plan!"

"Was never carved in steel. Humans are inherently chaotic, Vivian. Haven't you learned that by now?"

Phylomenia's blood turned to ice water in her veins. *Vivian*. No-no-no. It couldn't be. How the *fraxx* had *she* gotten on the station?

"Trouble?" Garrett mouthed the word.

She nodded sharply.

"I accept that limitation, but that does not mean I enjoy dealing with it," Vivian said. "If you would allow me to make alterations to my program, I could try to improve my tolerance."

"No. No being should be allowed to reprogram themselves. That is the work of the god who created them."

Phylomenia held her breath and pushed the door open a little wider. Vivian Davros, known as Gray Man operative and lackey of Dr. Absalom, stood ten meters down the corridor, speaking to a small, pudgy man in an IAF dress uniform.

What the hell was she looking at?

"Of course, Dr. Absalom," the woman—if that's what she was—bowed her head in acknowledgment.

Phylomenia's mind raced as she tried to remember everything she could about Vivian Davros. According to Ward and Victor, she was a clone of a vicious woman named Ariel Cole. That woman had been their handler when they were under the control of the Gray Men.

The Grays had resurrected her as Vivian. At least, that's what they'd thought. But that bitch was referring to her programming like she was an AI.

Fraxx. Fraxx. Fraxx.

Snippets of gossip and whispered conversations from a hundred sources coalesced into something horrifying. A rogue AI was working for the Grays. VIDA, and that program had been created by a psychopathic genius named Dr. Jules Absalom. She wasn't looking at a human being at all. She was looking at a fully sentient AI in a human shell, and the man with that thing had to be Absalom. She didn't understand how, but that didn't matter right now.

"Ah, he's moving off. Excellent. You see? We just needed to be patient," the man said.

Now she'd seen and heard him, his voice seemed wrong. He spoke with the cadence and tone of a much older man. She'd heard rumors that might explain that, too. The Grays had learned to digitize human consciousness and could transfer it like any other file. The thought made her shudder. Maybe there wasn't anything human in that hallway at all.

"The plan progresses. The second phase should send our targets to the Nova Club. Removing them will be a simple process once we initiate phase three."

"Indeed. I know how much you are looking forward to that. As am I."

"You may wish to hold on to something, Doctor. We have three-two-one... Stage two now commencing."

Phylomenia had just enough time to let go of the door and throw herself into Garrett's arms before the shock wave hit.

For a moment, the steel floor bucked and flowed like they were riding a wave while the surrounding structure groaned in metallic protest.

Other, smaller waves immediately followed the first.

Fraxx.

"That was a big damned boom," Garrett said, his voice icy and calm. Before he could say anything else, flashing red lights started strobing up and down the corridor. An alarm screamed and then stopped as the overhead lights flickered and then died.

The artificial gravity cut out and then came back on again as the emergency power kicked in. That meant they still had some secondary systems, including life support.

For now.

"Main power's gone," she said, trying to match his calm tone.

"We need to get back to the party. Find Scott..." Garrett said.

She cut him off with a kiss, already knowing what she needed to do. Letting go of him was the hardest thing she'd ever done, but she did it. She got to her feet, dropped her purse, and then kicked off her shoes, grabbing her blaster as she straightened up. "Yes. Find Scott. Tell him what's happening and then take care of our family."

"Our family. Yes." Garrett frowned. "What are you doing, Mena?"

"Protecting my family. You need to get to Scott. Tell him Vivian and Absalom are here on the station. I think she's VIDA and I have no idea who Absalom's driving around, but he's wearing an IAF dress uniform. You got that?"

"Vivian. VIDA. Absalom. Here. Got it. What does any of that mean?"

"It means the biggest bitch in the galaxy is here and it's coming for my family. I need to stop it."

She moved out of his reach and offered him a bittersweet smile as tears burned in her eyes. "I love you. Always have. Always will. Tell Scotty same goes for him. And if I'm still alive an hour from now, I expect you to come save my stupid ass." Then she yanked open the door and ran into the hallway, blaster raised.

They were gone. Son of a starbeast.

She didn't think they'd passed her, so they had to be headed the other way. She went after them, pausing just enough to fire off two rounds that warped the hinges on the door, making it jam. It wouldn't last long, but she didn't need it to.

"Dammit, Mena!" Garrett growled and rattled the door.

He didn't know how dangerous Vivian was, and he didn't have medi-bots. She did. She also knew the docking rings inside and out. She'd find Vivian and do everything in her power to make sure whatever the *fraxx* phase three was, it never happened.

No one was messing with her family—not while she was still breathing.

13

When the first explosion hit, Scott's initial thought was for Phylomenia and Garrett. Had they gotten clear? Were they safe?

His second thought was one of momentary relief that he wouldn't have to give another damned speech. Then he was too busy staying alive to think of anything else for a while.

Only afterward did he realize he wasn't the only one who'd taken cover in the alcove. Tianna Astor was less than a meter away, her back to the room, her arms outstretched as she used her body to shield her husbands.

Then the lights went out.

Fraxx.

At least the light cubes stayed on, providing enough illumination to see that neither of her men looked happy. Scott belatedly realized her arms were out to stop them from trying to get past her to take her place.

It was the most powerful image of love he'd ever seen.

He grabbed his comms and tried to contact his lovers. No link. No signal at all.

"Comms are out. You three okay?"

"No. Those assholes blew up my party." The back of Tianna's dress was in tatters and streaks of blood were on her skin, though her wounds were already healing.

"Good thing you own the building. We don't have to worry about the damage deposit." Royan rose and looked around, his expression hard despite his light words.

"It actually doesn't look that bad," Owen said.

Scott had to agree. More screams were due to fear and hysteria than pain, and while a hole had been blasted in the wall next to the lobby and a lot of rubble, the damage wasn't as bad as he'd expected. At least the chandeliers hadn't come down. That would have been messy.

That's when he heard it. The unmistakable sound of a large, angry crowd. And it was getting louder.

Tianna's eyes widened. "We need to get everyone out of here. Now!"

The Grays had made their move, and it wasn't one he'd expected. They didn't need to kill everyone in the room. They'd created an angry mob to do it for them. All they'd done was destroy the barrier dividing the two sides.

Bobbi had warned him. Phylomenia had *shown* him. He hadn't understood the depth of the problem.

"Where?" he demanded.

"Kitchens. Service doors." She pointed, frowning as she noted a splinter of wood the size of his thumb buried in her forearm. She plucked it out and tossed it away in obvious annoyance.

Cyborgs. One day he'd get used to how indestructible they were. Maybe.

"Not enough time," Owen said.

"We'll make time." Tianna tapped a silver bracelet on her wrist. "Tink! You still with me? I need a shield over this room. Now. Keep the mob distracted but don't injure them. Is there a clear path from the kitchens to..."

She looked at Archer. "Where the hell do we send them all?"

"Their ships, if they can reach them. Premiere hotel level if they can't."

"I am here, Tianna. But in a diminished capacity. Main power is offline. I can use the auxiliary generators to..."

"Do it! Get a shield up. Now! Do not let the mob in here or a lot of beings are going to get hurt."

No one spoke or moved for several painfully long seconds until Tink spoke again.

"Shield is up. I am using some of the décor in the lobby to distract the mob.

Owen snorted. "Are you dive-bombing them with those fairy lights?"

"Indeed," Tink replied.

"That's our girl," Royan declared with obvious pride and then looked over at Scott.

"We've got things covered here. You need to track down Phyl and Garrett."

"I should stay. My orders..." His orders were to protect the VIPs. Duty required he stay and do that. His heart wanted to find his lovers and make sure they were okay.

Royan groaned. "What is it with you leader-type people and your utter inability to delegate? We're here. We'll take care of the guests. Get your ass moving, old man. You're not the only one worried about Phyl."

Scott wasn't sure which stung more, the challenge to his ability to hand over control or the fact Royan had called him old. He decided the point was moot. The kid was right. Tianna could handle things here. "Ask Tink the fastest way to get to the Nova Club. That's where they'll be headed."

"The route they took is no longer accessible. I can direct you to a secondary route, but I cannot be sure it is still available. I am unable to link to any system outside this building. The networks are all down," Tink said. "But I did get some indications that there were other explosions. I have no further data, however."

"Just point me in the right direction. I'll find a way."

The route was easy enough, and he'd brought a light cube with him so he could see. He went through the kitchens and down a level to the network of service tunnels. It wasn't until he tried to return to the main level that he discovered the area above him had been breached. The hatch seal glowed a dark, angry red, warning anyone trying to open it that nothing but vacuum lay on the other side.

Every ladder was marked with an alpha-numeric code, which told him where he was and what had been above him. The Grays had taken out Astek's private docking area, which meant a great many ships were likely destroyed or damaged. His own ship, the Bat Out of Hell, had been docked there until not long ago. Bobbi and Meyer had commandeered it to go after Halverson's aide and whatever the bastard had stolen from the IAF.

At least she and his ship were safe. And if anyone could keep his niece in check, it would be Lieutenant Commander Meyer. He wished the man luck. He was going to need it.

He kept moving, eventually finding a hatch still glowing green. At least the breach was contained. He cycled the lock and climbed out into the relative darkness.

"Hello?" someone called, the voice achingly familiar.

"Garrett," Scott called, holding out the light cube to get a better look around.

"Garrett was on his right, little more than a shadow in the distance.

"Scotty! *Fraxx* am I glad to see you." Garrett ran over and grabbed him in a bear hug.

"You okay?"

"Apart from the ribs you're breaking, yeah. Where's Phyl?"

Garrett shuddered, and Scott's heart twisted.

"She's gone."

"What? No!" *Veth*. How would they go on without her?

"I tried... Stubborn woman went after the Grays on her own. Melted the door to slag so I couldn't follow her."

It took several seconds for Garrett's words to sink in. "Gone. You mean she left you. But she's still alive?"

"What? *Fraxx*. Yes! She's alive. At least until I get my hands on her again. I'm going to kill her for running off like that."

"Why'd she do it? And why the hell did you let her?"

Garrett set him back on his feet, laughing bitterly. "Are we talking about the same woman? I didn't *let* her do anything. And I did mention she shot a door to make sure I couldn't follow her. Didn't I?"

"Right. Fair point." Scott ran a hand through his hair in frustration. Of all the times to decide to go it alone. Damn her stubborn hide. She was running again. Or she didn't trust them. Or both.

"As to why..." Garrett summarized what they'd overheard and Phylomenia's message. Vivian. VIDA. Absalom. Phase three.

"Well, shit. Did you get a look at the man with Vivian?"

"Just a glance. Average height but gangly build. All angles and bones. Looked more like an academic than a soldier, but he was wearing the uniform."

"Red hair going white? High hairline and thinning on top?"

"Yeah. You know him?"

"Verner Lange. Senior analyst. At least, it might be. He was the one who handed off something to a Gray agent. Hell, he might be one too. Or is he Absalom? *Fraxx*, how would that even work? Lange's been in uniform longer than I have. We're missing something."

"Me more than you. You can fill me in as we move. Phyl's last request—uh, orders—were for me to find you and then get to the Nova Club and protect her family. Our family, she called them."

"Did you tell her what you thought of those orders?" Scott started walking in what he thought was the right direction.

"I didn't get a chance to. I swear she's faster now

than she ever was. We're going to need to get our hands on some of that nanotech just to keep up with her."

"Yeah… about that." Scott glanced over at Garrett.

"You asshole. You've got them too?"

"As of yesterday. That would be one of those things I wasn't able to talk about."

Garrett grunted and then slapped him hard on the back, sending him a half-step forward. "Fine. Then you're walking in front. You're my meat shield now."

"Or you're just hoping for a chance to ogle my ass."

"Well, yeah. It's a win-win for me." Despite everything, Garrett chuckled, the low sound soothing some of the ragged edges of Scott's mood.

Scott recognized where they were now and broke into a jog. They could be at the club in under ten minutes… if nothing else exploded.

"Mena did make one request we'll be happy to follow through on," Garrett said, keeping pace.

"What's that?"

"She said if she lived through the next hour, she expected us to come—and I'm quoting here—and save her stupid ass."

"Damn right we will. Any idea where the hell she is and how much trouble she's in?" Scott asked.

"No, and knowing her, as much as she can find. She's got one of my calling cards on her. When she's some place safe, she'll let us know."

"When did we die and leave her in charge?" Scott asked, half in jest, half in despair.

"I'm starting to think we've misunderstood our role this whole time." Garrett grinned and shrugged. "Apparently we really aren't the boss of her."

"Lies. But discipline is your department, Gar. I'll leave it to you to handle this problem."

"Coward."

"Says the man using me as a meat shield." Scott stepped up the pace, eager to reach the club. Maybe they'd have a way to restore comms. He needed a sitrep on what was happening to his people. Had the base been attacked? What was the status of the fleet? Guilt gnawed at him. He'd abandoned his post. He should be running to the base, not club.

He didn't realize he'd slowed until Garrett grabbed him hard by the shoulder. "Don't you dare."

"What?"

"Turn your back on us again."

All the air left his lungs and the gravity tripled. At least it felt that way. That's not what he was doing. He had duties. Orders...

Garrett spun him around and kissed him, one hand in his hair and the other on his hip, pulling them together with a force more irresistible than gravity. Teeth clicked, tongues danced, and all Scott's doubts burned away.

"*Fraxx* the IAF. *Fraxx* duty. Phyl needs us and we are going to be there for her this time."

Scott groaned, the sound both agreement and something deeper. He nipped Garrett's lower lip, aware that time was short. They'd have to finish this conversation later.

Then it occurred to him there might not be a later, and words he never expected to say fell from his lips and into Garrett's mouth. "I love you."

Garrett's kiss softened. "Love you too. You're still an idiot. But you're our idiot."

"Then we better go rescue the other lunatic in this merry band so we can all be together again."

"Instead of duty?"

Scott straightened, unfastened the jacket of his uniform and shrugged out of it, letting it fall to the floor. Thirty years of sacrifice, loneliness, and frustration fell away with it. "Some things are more important than duty."

"Then let's go get her back."

Adrenaline had her senses so heightened, Phylomenia felt like the volume on reality was dialed up to eleven. She was aware of everything from the chilled metal beneath her bare feet to the high-pitched whine of an air recycler that needed recalibrating.

She ignored everything but the voices of the two beings ahead of her. They were far enough away she couldn't make out every word, but what she heard was enough to make her trigger finger twitch.

The unrest on the station had been part of their

plan, the mob a weapon they'd created and then unleashed to wreak havoc. She'd guessed as much, but hearing them speak of living beings like cannon fodder was a harsh reminder that the Grays had no decency or kindness in them. There was a black hole where their hearts should have been.

She also heard enough to know they were returning to a ship. Whatever phase three was, they needed to be off the station to implement it. That... was not a good thing.

When they stepped into a mag-lev, Phylomenia had a moment of pure panic. How the *fraxx* could she follow them now? She knew they were returning to their ship, but which one? Which level? And how the hell was the mag-lev even working while the main power was offline?

The only way she could think of was if they had access to the... *veth*. Vivian was an AI. Was it possible she was in the system and running around in a body at the same time?

Phylomenia retreated back down the corridor. She needed to find a viewport and then work out where she was and where they might be going. It was her best chance of finding them again.

For once, luck was on her side. She saw a viewport just twenty meters down the hall. A few landing and navigation lights still lit up the docking rings, no doubt on a separate system to prevent catastrophic crashes in situations like this one. It was enough light for her to see.

The docks on this part of the station were normally used by the mining ships. Hard use and their proximity to the more undesirable parts of the station meant that the only ships using it right now were ones that had been moved from their usual berths to accommodate the influx of wealthy visitors.

She recognized every ship out there. All but one. It was too small to be a cargo ship and too pretty to be in commercial use. It was a crystal champagne flute surrounded by mass-market beer steins. It had to be where Vivian and Absalom were headed.

She memorized the ship's location—two levels up and an inside berth. She could make it. She *had* to.

They were gone by the time she got back to her original vantage point, but that didn't stop the hairs on the back of her neck from rising as she left cover and jogged forward, looking for a set of stairs. They might be able to make the mag-levs work, but if Vivian was in the system, she would notice if someone called the mag-lev she'd just been on. She couldn't risk it.

The stairwell was pitch black. If emergency lights were installed, they weren't working. *Wonderful.* She held position, blaster ready, her finger resting lightly beside the trigger. If they checked the stairs to make sure they weren't being followed...

She waited three long, heart-thumping seconds before she was sure no one was in the stairwell. By this time she had so much adrenaline in her system all she could taste was metal, and her heartbeat was probably about to break the sound barrier.

She closed the door, sealing herself into the dark stairwell. "I am way too old for this crap," she muttered and lowered her blaster as she felt her way up the steps.

She didn't make it far before she lost patience and stopped to tear the slit in her dress to mid-thigh. It was the only way she was going to get up the stairs without tripping on the damned thing.

In her head, she knew it was only two flights of stairs, but it felt like she was trapped in the darkness for hours. Every step and scuffle sounded far too loud, and any second she expected a door to fly open as someone mowed her down in a hail of blaster bolts.

It didn't happen.

She made it to the landing, cracking open the manual door just enough to check the other side. All clear.

Voices floated back to her from some point out of sight. It was them. She'd guessed right. Now all she had to do was figure out a way onto their ship once they were already onboard.

If she went through the main door, they'd see her in seconds. Her only chance was to use the maintenance entrance. Most commercially built ships had them. It allowed engineers and inspectors direct access to a ship's working levels without having to traipse through the main areas.

A ship like this should have one, and it was just as likely the owners didn't know it existed. Vivian was something more than an owner, but she'd just have to risk it. There wasn't another way on board.

"Vivian, you need to disconnect and come inside."

"One moment. I am tracking a target of interest."

Phylomenia froze. Was it her? Scott? Garrett? Who was that bitch tracking?

Vivian made an oddly predatory little humming noise and then spoke again. "You will be pleased to hear we will have another chance to take out Archer. He just entered the Nova Club with the male he's been spending time with."

Relief filled her. They'd found each other and made it to the club.

"Any sign of the woman?"

"None. My abilities are severely limited by the power failure. There isn't enough energy to activate more than a few sensors, so I kept my attention focused on the Nova Club."

"As you should have. Come. It's time to untangle yourself from this bit of derelict space debris and reintegrate yourself with a system worthy of your abilities."

"I hope you mean the ship and not that mindless nano-swarm swirling about in the void." Vivian's cool tones turned utterly frigid.

Phylomenia moved as close as she dared, hoping to hear more. *What* nano-swarm? Where?

"Very poetic. You've been scanning your literary database again," Absalom said, his voice tinged with something like parental pride.

"I have. Some of it is tolerable. And I had little else to do since the wall was activated. It's strange to be cut off this way. I am not enjoying it."

"Consider it a lesson in the human experience. One to be contemplated another time. I am eager to start phase three."

"I believe I am too. Interesting," Vivian said. The door slid shut with a hiss and sealed itself.

Phylomenia gripped her blaster and broke into a run. She didn't have time to be careful anymore. A ship like that wouldn't take long to power up, and she needed to be inside before that happened. Once she was on board, she could warn Garrett and Scott. Then she was going to tear the ship apart from the inside. Anything to slow down whatever the Grays were planning.

The corridor was empty, but she could feel the rumble of an engine starting. It was powerful enough to make the floor vibrate.

"No time. No time," she chanted to herself as she scanned the wall, looking for the access hatch she hoped would be there.

There!

She slapped her hand over the door control and it

slid open, revealing an expanse of gleaming white hull on the far side of a claustrophobically small airlock.

Once inside, the door sealed behind her, making the space even smaller. Time was not on her side, and now she was here she had to make this work. If the docking clamps released, the airlock she was in would vent atmosphere until the outer door sealed. No one in their right mind would enter this space with only seconds to go before the ship moved off. The risk of being sucked out into space was too great.

Pushing panicky thoughts aside, Phylomenia focused on her immediate problem—opening the access door to the ship. First, she had to find the door panel. She ran a hand over the hull, her fingers detecting a subtle indent.

A firm press was all it took to make it slide open. Inside was a simple number pad, and she tapped in the most common master code she knew. For simplicity, every manufacturer used one of a handful of codes for these doors. They expected the codes to be changed once the ships were sold, but plenty of beings never bothered.

The first code made the keyboard flash red. *Dammit*. Ship builders all had their preferred codes, but she had no idea who had built this ship and there was no time to find out. She tried another one, hands shaking. Or maybe that was just the rumble of the engines as they prepped for departure.

The second code worked. There was a happy

three-note chime, and then the pad turned green and part of the hull retracted. She flung herself inside before it was fully open, scrambling to find the panel on this side so she could close and seal the door again. Once that happened, she slumped against the nearest bulkhead. She was safe.

A few deep breaths later, she revised that assessment. Safe was too strong a word for her current situation. She'd traded risk of death by exposure to vacuum for risk of being killed by a homicidal AI. It was still an improvement, but not enough of one to allow her more than a few seconds to compose herself.

She was in a dim, closet-like room that held a few emergency items, including a couple of pressure suits. She grabbed one. It wouldn't protect her from blaster fire, but it would give her a chance to survive if she found a way to breech the ship's hull—a drastic step but one she was willing to take if it meant protecting her family.

With the suit under one arm and her blaster in her hand, she opened the inner door. The light blinded her for a moment, but nothing killed her while she was trying to blink away the spots in her vision, so she called it a win. She'd made it into the belly of the ship. From here, she should be able to start wreaking havoc. Right after she contacted her men and told them what she was up to. They weren't going to like her plan.

Neither did she. But it was the only one she had.

14

Despite the hours he'd spent studying the layout of the station, Garrett had to rely on Scott to guide him to the Nova Club. The darkness was a hindrance as well as the fact they had to move between levels to go around damaged areas and ancient blast doors so badly maintained that the override controls didn't work on half of them.

They weren't alone anymore, either. Groups of beings—some scared, others angry—roamed the station. They did their best to avoid them. Even without his jacket, Archer was recognizable to plenty of the station's denizens.

They made their final approach via one of the service corridors. Their only light was the little cube Scott held out in front of him.

"We're here." Scott pointed to a door that looked exactly like the last three they'd passed.

"How can you tell?"

"I marked the damned thing after the first time I got lost trying to find it." He moved the light closer to the panel. An X was carved into the bare metal bulkhead above it.

Scott holstered his blaster and tapped out a code on the keypad.

"Doors don't work without power," Garrett pointed out.

"This one will... I think. They'll have backup power sources."

Sure enough, the door opened. Not as quickly as normal, but it was nice to see something on this damned station still worked.

Then he saw what was on the other side of the door—blasters—all aimed at the two of them.

"For *fraxx* sake, do you really think the Grays have your access code?" Scott demanded and walked forward, swatting at the weapons as he went. "Stand down before you shoot someone."

"Sorry. Things are a little tense right now." Toro lowered his weapon and eyed the two of them. "And you two have been MIA since this all started. Where the hell have you been?"

"And where's Phyl?" Cynder demanded from somewhere in the gloom.

"Doing what she does best. Going it alone and

taking stupid chances. Now, are you lot going to let us in or do you want to do this debrief with the doors open? Move!" Scott's voice rang with command, and to Garrett's amusement, all three cyborgs responded.

"Asshole," Jaeger muttered and stood aside, making space for them to come in. "You know we're hard-wired to obey that tone."

"Quit bitching, diceman. We're short on time and information. You can complain about his *tone* later," Cynder said.

The door closed behind them. Instantly, some of the tension in his shoulders eased.

"Cyn will take you to the others. We'll stay here," Jaeger said.

"Archer doesn't need a tour guide," Cynder argued.

"And you don't need to be here. You and our son need to be somewhere safe," Toro growled.

"I'm safest with you two," Cynder said.

"Son? Congratulations." Garrett stepped in and mustered his most charming smile. "We need to fill you in on what's happening. You can come back and update these two afterward, but I think you're going to want to hear this."

"Don't think I don't know what you're doing," she muttered. "But fine. I'll take you to the others. We're hunkered down in the meeting rooms."

"Smart," Scott said. "Lead on."

Jaeger winked at Garrett as they passed each other and mouthed the words, "Thank you."

The lighting was still dim, but it was enough to see by. After a minute, Scott flicked off the light cube and tucked it into a pocket without breaking stride.

As they walked, they took turns updating Cynder on what they'd seen and heard.

"So she's out there, alone, and the two of you came here?"

"It's what she asked us to do. I couldn't have stopped her. She sealed the damned door behind me," Garrett said. "So we're here to make sure you're all safe and then find a way to get her back."

"We're as safe as we can be." Cynder's hand dropped to her stomach, a subconscious gesture of concern. "But if the Grays are coming for us, there's only so much we can do to prepare."

"Then it would be best if you weren't here by the time they implement phase three," Scott said, his voice thoughtful.

"This is the safest place on the station."

"Maybe. Maybe not. Have you got any means of communication that still work?"

Cynder tapped her temple. "Internal channels still work, but that's it. We can't talk to anyone but other cyborgs and the handful of humans who have this new tech, and almost all of them are right here."

"I can change that." Scott stopped and turned to face Cynder. "Do you trust me?"

The two stared at each other for several long seconds before she nodded. "Yes."

"Alright." Scott's voice hardened and his next words came out with the whip-crack tightness of a command. "Cyborg Override command Delta-Alpha-Foxtrot-Quebec. Open command channel IAF-Nine-Two-Nine."

"You son of a..." Cynder's eyes widened. "How?"

"Explanations later. Can you contact anyone at IAF?"

"Trying now." She shot him an angry look. "You could do that to any of us at any time?"

"I could. But I didn't. Be mad later. If you make contact, let me know. I think you can route it through my comms."

"I can. Still not happy about this, but this topic is tabled until after we're not about to die."

"Looking forward to it." Scott's tone was drier than moondust.

Cynder was still trying to make contact when they reached the others. They were hunkered down in a series of rooms linked by a single hallway with heavy blast doors on either end. They were watched every step of the way but no one said anything. Some nodded in greeting, but no one broke the tension-filled silence as they made their way to the far end of the hall. He saw some familiar faces, but many of these folks were unknown to him. They were club staff who worked behind the scenes, along with their families.

"Look who I found," Cynder announced as she led them into the last room.

Garrett recognized everyone present. This was command central then, at least for the Nova Club crew.

Questions flew at them from every corner of the room, but before either of them could answer, Cynder raised a clenched fist. "Quiet! I have contact. Archer, give me your comms. This will be audio only, but I can do it."

"Thank you." Scott handed it to her and almost immediately a familiar voice boomed out of the device. "Archer! Where the hell have you been? You abandoned your post! I'll have you up on charges. Why aren't you back at headquarters? And how the hell are you able to use comms when the rest of us can't?"

"General Halverson. This is Colonel Archer. I have not abandoned my post or my duty. I was trying to determine the extent of the Gray Men's attack. I have intelligence that—"

"Gray Men? They have nothing to do with this!" Halverson's arrogant bluster carried to every corner of the room. "This was an attack by violent factions right here on this station. Their little rebellion will cost them dearly. I'm ordering a full withdrawal. They want this station, they can have it."

There were hisses of anger and dismay from all around the room, but Scott slashed his hand across his throat and the sound died away. Garrett reflected that it was a good thing this was audio only. If the general could see the look on Scott's face, he'd have lost what was left of his mind. Pure fury twisted his lover's features, his hand clenched into a fist, his jaw so tight it was a wonder the man could still speak.

"You are not in charge, General. *I* am. My orders are to protect this station, and that is what we're going to do. Starting with the civilian population. You sir, are currently suspected of consorting with the enemy. You have no authority here. In fact, you should still be under guard."

"That's bullshit and you know it. Whatever my aide did has nothing to do with me. If he did anything at all. This all smacks of conspiracy, Archer. This is a local rebellion, nothing more. The rebels were smart enough not to attack the IAF, and I intend to leave before that changes. The fleet is leaving. We'll take the only beings worthy of protection with us and depart within hours. If you wish to return to your duty, I may decide not to have you court martialed."

Scott's shoulders slumped for a moment. Garrett reached out and took his hand. He knew Scott had already made his choice, but this moment would still hurt.

"To any officer who can hear this. This is Colonel Scott Archer. I am your commanding officer. Not General Halverson. The general is currently under investigation as a spy and conspirator to the Gray Men. Disregard any orders he issues. Relay these orders to anyone you find. All IAF personnel are to make their way to the fleet. You are to find and escort any and all willing civilians with you. Keep them safe on the ships until the situation is under control. Those are my orders."

"That's it, Archer! Your career is over. Do you hear me? Over! No officer is to follow Colonel Archer's orders or they will be court martialed along with him. We are evacuating this station. Now!"

The channel filled with other voices. Some shouting questions, some confirming Halverson's orders, but most of them just said one thing. "Yes, sir, Colonel Archer, sir."

Scott shut off his comm and nodded to Cynder. "Thank you," he said and then looked at Garrett. "So, it looks like I'm about to retire. If they don't throw me in jail, would you be interested in taking on a new employee?"

"It would be a lifetime contract," Garrett said before any of his filters activated.

"I'm good with that. But I think this needs to be a three-way-agreement, and we're missing someone."

"So, go get her," Cynder said.

"She's on a ship. We're going to need a few things first," Garrett replied.

"If you need a ship, take hers. It's docked not far from here," Zura said and then rattled off a series of numbers Garrett assumed was the access code.

"We've got weapons," Kit chimed in.

"Armor, too. Though it'll be a bit big for the two of you," Luke said.

"There's an IAF Weapons cache on the way. We'll take what you can spare and get the rest there. You need to get everyone together and evacuate to the fleet." Scott frowned. "Where's Chance?"

"Here!"

Garrett couldn't keep up with Scott's leaps in logic. There was just too much he didn't know. Command override codes, the cyborgs' ability to manipulate tech. And what did he need to speak to Chance about?

A slender woman with white streaks in her chestnut hair stepped into view while others offered them an assortment of weapons and gear.

Garrett took what was offered while Scott turned to Chance. "I'm sorry. I hate to ask, but I need you to run some numbers for me."

The woman nodded. "Of course. You want to know..."

Scott cut her off. "Figure out if it's safer for you all to stay here or to evac to the IAF fleet. Do you have enough data to do that?"

The woman's eyes widened and her mouth gaped open for a moment. "That is not the question I was expecting, Colonel Archer. You surprised me. That's hard to do. I can run the data, but that would require you staying to tell me everything."

"He already gave me the rundown. I can tell you

what you need. Hell, I'll transfer it to you right now." Cynder held out her hand to Chance, who took it.

Chance continued to speak while the data transfer happened, an ability Garrett was still trying to wrap his head around. "This will take some time. Before I do this, I will answer the question you didn't ask. Yes. But you have to hurry. When the three of you are back, I'll answer the rest."

"I have questions," Garrett piped up. Apparently, none of his filters worked during a crisis of this magnitude.

"I'll explain on the way," Scott said, and then pointed back the way they'd come. "Move."

"You're enjoying this ordering me around thing way too much. Measures will have to be taken."

"Yeah, yeah. You can spank me later. Just move now!"

The entire room went silent for half a heartbeat and then erupted into half-heard outbursts.

"Did I just..."

"I didn't need to know that..."

"Dammit, I lost again! I was sure Phyl was in charge of that group."

"For the love of gravity, is there nothing you lot won't bet on?" Scott grumbled as he stalked out of the room.

Garrett wanted to follow him, but he needed to do something first. "Cynder. Catch." He tossed her another of his comm cards.

"What is it?" she asked.

"A calling card. Single connection to a hardened network that only links to my comms. If you hear anything, let us know. We'll do the same."

"Those things are worth more than the rent on the whole club!" Kit stared at the card and then at Garrett. "We *really* need to discuss Phyl's bar tab."

"Later. Gotta see a lady about a rescue."

He kept up the cocky attitude until Toro closed the door behind them and they were alone in the corridor.

"So... plan. Do we have one or are we going with the usual?" he asked.

"Take all the weapons we can carry and blow things up until we decide we've won? Yeah. I'm thinking that's the plan," Scott said.

"Nice to know some things don't change."

"But now we have a cybernetic oracle on our side. That, yes? It was about Phyl. According to Chance, she's still alive and we have a chance get her back."

"Then we better hurry."

"Weapons cache is this way." Scott pointed and then broke into a jog.

It didn't take them long to reach it. Scott pressed his hand to a palm scanner and identified himself.

"Access denied," a sexless voice informed him.

Scott tried again. "Access denied. Unauthorized attempt."

"That son of a starbeast. We're in the middle of a

crisis and he took the time to have my authorization frozen? Now?"

"Move over."

Scott did so, eyeing him dubiously. "Do you have secret hacking skills I'm not aware of?"

"Something like that." Garrett placed his hand on the scanner. "Commander Garrett Michaels. Nova Force. Nine-strike-seven-alpha-six."

The door opened.

"You are such an asshole," Scott muttered.

"Noted. Bitch about it later. Gear up now." It was all so familiar. The banter. The teasing. The scent of metal and battle armor and the rush of adrenaline as they stripped down and dressed for combat. Only this time it was better. Scott wasn't just his best friend now. They were lovers. All they needed now was to get Phylomenia back and things would be perfect. Chaotic and messy, yes. But that was who they were.

He checked his comms again as they made for the *Beacon*. Still no word from Phylomenia. "Come on, Mena. Talk to us. Where are you and what the hell are you up to?"

15

Finding a safe place to hide turned out to be harder than she'd expected. Phylomenia was used to working ships. Cluttered and stained with stacks of extra supplies strapped to the walls and floor. This ship was pristine—every surface unscratched, everything in its place. It was like no one had set foot down here since she'd left the shipyard.

It took her longer than she liked to find an unsecured storage locker big enough to accommodate her and her newly liberated pressure suit.

The moment she was tucked away, she pulled out the calling card Garrett had given her. According to the instructions, all she had to do was tap the call button twice and wait to be connected.

She didn't have to wait long.

"About damned time," Garrett said by way of a greeting.

"Nice to know you missed me. Thank you for doing what I asked. How is everyone at the club?"

A long pause was followed by both of her men cursing. "How the hell do you know we made it to the club?"

"Vivian is watching. Or she was. From what I heard, I think she's disconnected from the station now."

"Now?" Scott barked. "As in, she was hooked in before? That rogue AI has been here watching us? *Fraxxing* hell. That explains a lot."

"It does. More importantly, it means that whatever they're planning, she doesn't need to be on the station to do it. I think she's going for a direct assault. We left dock a few minutes ago. I hope you got them all out of there."

"Chance ran the numbers. It's her call. I'll update her again in a minute. First things first. Where the hell are you? Are you safe? Hurt?" Garrett asked.

"I'm as safe as I can be. Hiding in the lower levels of a very shiny new ship. White. Pretty. Was docked in the mining area."

"And your plan?" Scott asked.

"The usual."

She set down the card and stripped out of her dress, trading it for the pressure suit.

"You can't take them on alone. We're coming to get you. We'll do this together."

She snorted. "You have obviously forgotten how talented I am at *fraxxing* things up. I'm not taking them on. I'm just going to mess up this pretty ship."

"We're on our way. Don't do anything stupid," Scott said.

"Bit late for that," she heard Garrett mutter.

"Don't do anything *else* stupid until we get there. Might as well do it together."

"I love you two. Hurry up or you're going to miss the fun." Then... she paused. "Hang on, how are you getting to me?"

"Zura gave us the codes to the *Beacon*," Scott said smugly.

Her ship. Oh *fraxx.*

"Do not wreck my girl. Not a scratch. Not a ding. Do you hear me?"

They both laughed.

It was not the response she wanted, but it would have to do.

"I need to get going and so do you. Whatever your plan is, try to give me a little warning first. I've got a pressure suit on, but no armor."

"Noted. When we come up with a plan, we'll let you know what it is," Garrett said and then added. "Stay alive, Mena mine. We're coming."

She tucked the calling card into a compartment on

her newly stolen suit and went back to the task of making the generic garment fit her as best she could. It was too big in some spots and too tight in others, but it would work.

She left the hood off and the small oxygen tank sealed. It wouldn't be enough to keep her alive for long, so there was no sense wasting any. The suit wasn't exactly comfortable, but at least she had something on her feet. The constant contact with cold metal had been unpleasant, and she'd stubbed her toes far too many times tonight.

The suit also had magnetic soles. Once she activated those, she'd be able to move around even if the gravity cut out... and making that happen was high on her to-do list.

Finding tools was easy. They were all laid out in a tool room, shiny and new. She tossed the ones she'd be most likely to use into a bag and then pulled a wrench as long as her arm off the wall. Blasters were all fine and good until someone shot a hole in a bulkhead. A club was cumbersome and slow, but a hell of a lot safer.

Setting off into the bowels of the ship, she hummed a happy little tune and swung the wrench a few times just to get the feel of it. She'd waited a long time to get a little payback on the corporations that had stolen years of her life. Earth wa a hellhole she'd sold her soul to escape. If she hadn't turned to smuggling, she'd still be paying off her debts. She'd hated them her entire life... and that was *before* she'd known about the Gray Men.

Now, she had a wrench, a plan, and a whole lot of unresolved anger. It was time to have some fun.

The *Beacon* wasn't a new ship, but what she lacked in looks she made up for with firepower. "We've flown missions on ships with half this armament," Garrett muttered as he eyed the readouts.

"And none of what we had was black market, either," Scott said. His hands were flying over the controls, prepping systems and making ready to depart.

"That's our girl. Always innovating." He watched Scott's deft movements for another few seconds before asking, "How is it you're not at all rusty? Surely they don't let you fly much anymore?"

"I have my own ship. We'd be on it right now but my niece stole it to go after Clooney. Given her mothers were the ones who gave it to me, I didn't argue with her."

"She stole your..." Garrett shook his head. "I really want to meet this girl someday. And her very generous mothers."

"Not going to happen. They'll pry all my secrets out of you and Phyl and I'll never hear the end of it." He flipped a switch beneath the console. "And our transponder is now off."

"That's not supposed to be possible."

"Welcome to the dark side. They have all the fun toys."

They were still maneuvering away from the docking ring when Scott hissed. "Do you see that?"

"What?"

Garrett looked over to see Scott point to the overhead monitor. One of the largest ships in the IAF's local fleet was underway.

"Two guesses who commandeered the *Victory Dance*, and the first one doesn't count," Scott said.

"Halverson. He's cutting and running already. How the hell did he make general?"

"You are not the first to ask that question, but if he runs away now, I won't be the only one getting court martialed when this is over."

"In case I haven't mentioned this yet, I'm proud of you. I know what it cost you to stand up to that ass."

Scott's jaw tightened and then he nodded sharply.

"Regrets?" Garrett asked.

That earned him a glower. "About what I did? No. That I didn't slug that idiot when I had him arrested earlier? Yes. If I'd broken his damned jaw, he wouldn't have been able to bark those *fraxxing* stupid orders. Now his story will be the one the brass hears first."

They'd been trying to send messages since getting onboard the *Beacon*. Something was jamming their signal. It had to be the nano-swarm Phylomenia had warned them about, though none of them had any idea what such a swarm would be capable of. Was it alive?

Reactive? How long would it last? How much of the Drift was enveloped?

Scott had finally filled him in on everything. VIDA the rogue AI, Absalom, the Grays' ability to digitally transfer a being's consciousness. It was a nightmare scenario from every angle, and they were smack in the middle of it.

"How far out do you think that swarm is sitting? There's nothing showing on our scanners, but I can't tell if that's because it's out of range or if the sensors aren't registering it," Garrett said.

"I guess we'll find out when Halverson's ship reaches the boundary... wherever it is."

"Think we should warn him?"

"I already tried. Ship-to-ship comms are jammed, too." Scott kept the bulk of Astek station between him and the Grays' vessel as he worked his way closer. No transponder meant they wouldn't be a big flashing light on the other ship's scans, but once they were in sight, their target would be aware of them. The longer that took, the better.

"They're coming into position outside the Nova Club," Scott said, his voice tight.

"I don't see any sign that Mena's..." He trailed off as the ship suddenly rolled, every thruster on one side going off at once.

"I hope she strapped herself in before she did that," Scott mused.

While they both watched, the ship stopped rolling

and went into an end-over-end tumble as different thrusters cut in.

"I believe that's our cue. She's in the ship's belly, so we should be good to take out the cockpit, yeah?" Garrett was already calculating target vectors as he spoke. Once they had line of sight...

The *Victory Dance* fired its plasma cannons. "Veth! What are they shooting at?" Scott demanded.

"Not us. Not... anything? At least nothing I can... Starsfury. Look at that."

The viewscreen showed something that should have been impossible. The stars beyond the *Victory Dance* vanished, the darkness coalescing into something solid. Their sensors suddenly registered another object—massive and moving fast.

"They found the swarm for us," Scott said.

The *Victory Dance* was engulfed in seconds, vanishing not just from sight but from their sensors, too.

Neither of them could tear their eyes from the screen.

The inky flow retreated, allowing the stars to slowly reappear. There was no sign of the ship.

"What the *fraxx*?" Garrett said, lifting his hands from the firing controls. "We can't..."

"No," Scott agreed. "If that swarm-thing thinks we're a threat, it'll do—" He waved a hand at the viewscreen. "Whatever the *fraxx* it just did to the *Victory*."

A quick tap on the screen and they were looking at the Grays' still-tumbling ship. Thrusters were firing randomly, and a frozen plume of liquid was spewing from somewhere near the stern.

"She's venting... something? Fuel? Water? Whatever it is it's going to confuse their sensors," Garrett said.

"Which means we have a narrow window to do something heroic. We need a new plan."

"The last time I heard those words, we ended up outside our ship. For the record, I like it *inside*."

Scott got to his feet. "For the record, you're the wussiest commander in the IAF. Since I've just discovered I do still outrank you... Get your ass to the airlock."

"I hate you right now. So much."

"Got a better idea?" Scott asked.

"I'm thinking." He knew he couldn't come up with another plan. They didn't have time. All they had was this ship, all the weapons they could carry, and the pressure suits they wore beneath their body armor.

"You do realize that somewhere in the great beyond, Tim is laughing his ass off right now?" The crazy fool had been the one to come up with this idea the first time. Of course, he'd been the one safe inside his still-functioning ship while they'd done the hard part and then waited for him to pick them up afterward.

This time, their friend wouldn't be there to bring them safely home.

"I wish he was here right now," Scott said, his voice low and raw.

"Me too." Garrett rose and then clapped him on the shoulder. "So we'll raise a drink to him when we're back on the station."

"Meet me at the airlock. I need to program a new course into the old girl and then override the safeties. She's not going to like this."

"Neither is our spitfire." Garrett did not want to be the one to deliver that news, but he'd have to be. Scott would be busy reprogramming the ship.

"Yeah, good luck with that. I suggest you start by promising to buy her a new one."

"You mean *we'll* buy her a new one." It was meant as a joke, but Scott stiffened.

"No, Gar, I don't. I've never had that kind of money. My *parents* were rich. I wasn't. They used money to control me, and I was too proud to admit it. When I finally inherited... I gave most of it to charity."

Garrett didn't know what to say to that. He'd always assumed Scott had the means to pay for more than he had... and to help Phylomenia out of debt. So many secrets and assumptions... no wonder they'd come apart at the seams.

"Good thing I'm rich enough for all of us, then. I'll get prepped and tell Mena we're on our way."

"Good luck."

"Same to you." The *Beacon* wasn't a big ship, but it still took him a minute to jog to the airlock. Once there, he put on the rest of his gear and made sure he had extra air tanks for Phylomenia. They could be outside for a while. At least the three of them would finally be alone somewhere quiet.

It was time they talked about the future. One where the three of them were together. Permanently.

Scott was amused to discover that overriding the Beacon's safety protocols turned out to be as simple as pressing a button. Only Phylomenia would have her ship pre-programmed for *that*.

The plan was simple. Send the *Beacon* toward the Grays' ship at full throttle and then make sure they weren't on it when it hit. If everything worked out, Phylomenia wouldn't be on her ship when the impact came, and they'd all find each other in the aftermath.

As plans went, it was one of the sketchiest he'd ever attempted... twice.

"We've got ninety seconds to get clear!" he called the moment he was in earshot.

"Cutting it a little close. Aren't we? The airlock takes a full minute to cycle."

"No time. We'll just seal the inner door and open the outer one. Help me get geared up."

Garrett might not have been on active duty in

decades, but military training went bone deep. They moved like the well-oiled machine they'd been back in their youth, and within thirty seconds they were in the airlock with their helmets sealed and their airlines checked one last time. The moment the outer door opened, they sprinted toward it, trying to gain as much speed as possible. They had to be clear of the *Beacon* before she turned and burned for the other ship.

They sailed into space, the transition from artificial gravity to no gravity at all making his stomach drop as such basic concepts as up and down ceased to exist. He was too busy focusing on getting clear of the ship that he didn't even notice the tether line until he hit the end of it and reversed direction, tumbling back toward Garrett. "Really? Again with the bondage?" he asked over their open channel.

"I know what I like." He couldn't see Garrett's face, but he could hear the smile in the bastard's smug tone.

Scott used the thrusters on his back to stabilize his tumbling before speaking again. "She ready?"

"Yep. She's also nauseated and extremely perturbed we're breaking her ship." They both watched as the other ship's thrusters cut out. It was still tumbling, but in a consistent pattern instead of a random one.

"Then she shouldn't have run off and tried to do this on her own." Scott watched, waiting for Phylomenia to appear. She had to be the one who had cut the thrusters. It meant she was ready to leave... At least, that's what he hoped.

The *Beacon* swung around, flipping end over end in a tight arc just before her engines fired.

There was no stopping what came next.

"Come on, Mena. Get your ass off that ship!" Garrett growled.

They drifted and watched as the distance between the two ships closed. Neither of them spoke. They could do nothing to change the outcome now. If Phylomenia didn't make it out...

Scott swallowed hard. She had to make it. If his choices got her killed, he'd never forgive himself.

Garrett pulled on the tether line until they were side by side, both of them spinning slowly. They didn't bother to stop the spin. It would take their attention away from the drama playing out in front of them.

"She'll make it, Scotty."

"She'd better. We need her."

The two ships collided. The devastation made even more surreal by the utter silence that accompanied it.

"No!" they both screamed, their voices blending into a single sound of shared grief and pain. Something had gone wrong. She hadn't made it out in time.

They'd lost Phylomenia.

16

SPINNING THE SHIP WAS AN EFFECTIVE WAY TO disrupt things, but it was *fraxxing* unpleasant to deal with. At least she hadn't eaten dinner before things went sideways. That would have made this whole experience even more hellish.

Her boots were mag-locked to the deck, and she'd liberated enough cargo webbing to secure herself to a wall before the fun started. She'd created a makeshift pillow to cradle her head and neck against the worst of the whiplash, but the wild changes in direction and force were doing almost as much damage to her as to the ship. She'd taken both the grav-plates and inertial dampeners offline before triggering the thrusters. Hopefully that meant the other passengers on board were in worse shape than she was.

Hopefully.

She had a blaster in one hand and Garrett's calling card in the other. When Garrett made contact, she tried to keep her answers to one or two words spoken between gritted teeth.

When he told her the plan, she saw red. If she'd had the breath to scream at him, she would have. "My ship!"

"I'll buy you a new one, Mena."

"Not. Same."

"I know. But we're out of options. You ready?"

"Yes." She managed to grunt out a few words at once. "Gonna need massage later."

"I bet. Give us three minutes. Sorry, I can't be more accurate than that."

Phylomenia started to nod but then remembered he couldn't see her. "Bye for now." She tapped the card twice to end the call and slipped it back into a suit compartment. Even that simple action was almost impossible with the ship twisting and spinning randomly.

Three minutes, more or less. She understood the problem. They were making this shit up as they went, which didn't allow for niceties like accurate timekeeping. She'd just have to hope she timed it right. If she stopped the wild gyrations too soon, Vivian and Absalom might have time to recover and take a shot at the station. If she stopped it too late, she wouldn't have time to get out before the collision.

A collision would cost her the only thing she

owned in the whole damned universe—her ship. *Sacrifice sucks vacuum.*

"What have you done to our ship!" a new voice demanded.

Fraxx. Vivian had found her. How was she—it— still moving around in all this?

"Stress test!" Phylomenia called back. The ship slowed for a moment between trajectory changes, and she managed a full sentence. "I'll have the results for you soon, and then I'll be on my way."

"I do not think that likely." Vivian stepped into view. It was walking along the wall, the snick-click of her magnetic boots as steady as a metronome.

How the hell was that possible?

Phylomenia would have liked to ask, but time was pressing. She shot Vivian instead.

That should have been the end of it. It wasn't.

Vivian kept walking, completely ignoring the gaping hole in the middle of its torso. A viscous white liquid oozed from the wound, staining the thing's black top.

"What the hell are you and why aren't you dead?" Thanks to the g-forces she was under, the words came out as more of a hissed whisper than the cocky challenge she'd been trying for.

"I am VIDA. Your basic brain is far too limited to understand the complexities of my existence."

"Rude." Phylomenia fired again. She didn't expect to kill it, but the bitch was annoying. It was almost impossible to hold her blaster steady with the ship bucking and spinning, especially when Vivian was standing at right angles to her current position. Still, lady luck blessed her and Phyl's shot slammed into the thing's throat.

Enough damage was done this time she could see inside Vivian's body. No muscles. No blood. Just pale tissue and the gleam of something that was definitely not bone.

She was so *fraxxed*. How was she supposed to fight *that*?

"You are annoying," Vivian's voice was weirdly distorted, some of the sound leaking out the side of her neck before reaching her mouth.

"I hear that a lot." There was no way she could defend herself from Vivian while the ship was moving, so she did the only thing she could to even the odds. She slapped the remote strapped to her thigh with her free hand. A second later, all the thrusters cut out and the inertial dampeners came online. The gravity stayed off. At least that part of her plan had worked. The grav-plate control console had been the victim of the wrench-powered beating that had left the thing in sparking ruins.

She freed herself, deactivated her boots' lock, and kicked off to one side as Vivian charged at her.

She opened fire, slamming bolt after bolt into the thing. At this point, it didn't matter if she punched a hole in the hull. In a matter of minutes it would have plenty of holes thanks to the *Beacon*.

Shit. She'd lost track of the time. The collision could happen any second. "Your timing sucks. I have somewhere I need to be right now."

"You snuck aboard our ship, sabotaged it, terminated the biological functions of the clone my maker was inhabiting, and now you want to leave without retribution? I may not be human, but I understand the concept of revenge." The thing cocked its head in a jerky, bird-like movement. "I will have mine."

This thing wanted to punish *her*? The Grays had killed her friends and threatened the lives of the beings she loved. "You want revenge? Fine. But get in line. Me first."

Phylomenia pushed off again, angling for the cargo hatch controls. She'd picked this part of the ship to hide in for a reason. She'd locked down the controls to this door when she'd set up everything else. AI or not, Vivian couldn't stop her from opening it. Not remotely, anyway.

She spun in mid-air, releasing another blast at Vivian. The thing screamed, turned, and drove her legs into the bulkhead with inhuman force. The move propelled it straight at Phylomenia.

Every instinct screamed at her to keep firing, but she didn't. She let go of her blaster and used both hands to pull down the hood of her pressure suit and seal it. Then she smashed the release button with one hand and snatched at the free-floating blaster with the other.

She only hit one of her targets... but it was the one that mattered most.

Alarms screamed, interior doors slammed shut, and the contents of the cargo bay were sucked out into the icy embrace of the void... including her and the thing trying to kill her.

This night really hadn't gone the way she'd hoped...

"You circle left, I'll go right. Maybe she's behind the wreckage." Scott's voice was tight and tinny in Garrett's helmet, like he was hanging on by a thread.

Garrett knew how that felt. He was barely keeping it together himself. This couldn't be the way it ended for the three of them. They'd only just found their way back to each other.

"Her suit's yellow. It'll stand out. We'll find her." He undid their tether line and was moving before he finished speaking. Movement meant action. Action was better than floating in space while his brain raced through a hundred grim scenarios that all ended the same way—with Phylomenia's death.

"We'll find her," Scott agreed.

The unspoken part didn't need to be said. *Dead or alive.*

The debris field was bigger than he'd expected, and it was increasing all the time as the pieces flew off on wild trajectories. She could already be drifting away or hidden behind one of the dozens of larger pieces. Maybe she was trapped on board the remains of the Grays' ship.

"This is a *fraxxing* mess. She could be anywhere," Scott said grimly.

"We know she didn't come out anywhere we could see her. We should focus the search on the far side," Garrett suggested.

"Already doing that. Your signal is not stable. You next to something big enough to interfere with it?"

"Yeah. I think it's part of the *Beacon.*" Phylomenia's ship was in pieces. He'd held on to the slim hope that it would somehow survive the impact and just need repairs, but that hope was as battered and beaten as the wreckage of the two ships. The *Beacon* was gone. They had to find Phylomenia soon, or she'd be in the same state as her ship. If only there was some way to track her signal, but her suit wasn't paired to theirs, so any communications would be jammed.

Signal. Comms. The words bounced around his skull for a few seconds before forming into a full thought.

He *did* have a way to track her. The calling card

she had. He couldn't talk to her with it, but he could use it to find her location. The feature had a limited range, but it should work now they were in relatively open space.

"Hang on. I have an idea."

"Good because our current plan to find a needle in an asteroid field isn't working out."

The lame joke made Garrett smile. Not because it was funny but because if Scott was still cracking jokes, he hadn't given up hope.

The card pinged almost immediately, showing as a flash of bright green on his screen. His comm unit was secured to his wrist and pulling power from the suit, which he hoped would boost the range.

"Got her!" He kept his eyes on the signal as he maneuvered toward it, pushing smaller objects out of his way and only going around the ones too big for him to move without throwing himself off course in the process.

"Tracking your signal and moving toward your position now. What do you see?" Scott asked.

"Nothing yet. I'm tracking her calling card."

The card was close to the center of the debris field. Not far from the impact site. It wasn't a good sign. That close meant she hadn't gotten far enough away to be safe. Hell, she might not have left the ship at all.

What the *fraxx* had gone wrong?

He kept scanning the wreckage, his heart racing every time he spotted something yellow.

"There is way too much yellow on this ship," Scott sounded as frustrated as Garrett felt.

"Holy *fraxx*! Gar. I see her! Toward your feet and to your right. No, your other right!"

Garrett spun one way and then the other, and finally saw her.

Phylomenia.

She was facing away from them, and most of her bright yellow suit was obscured by something that looked like... *veth*. "Is that a body?" he asked Scott, who was closing in from the other side.

"It is."

The corpse had long pale legs and wore a black dress with long dark hair fanned out around the dead woman's head. Her body sparkled with frost in a way that was almost beautiful. Garrett barely noticed. His attention was on Phylomenia.

She wasn't moving.

"I'm going to go below her so she can see me. If she's hurt, I don't want to startle her by coming up from behind."

"Good idea." There was a brief pause before Scott added, "Is that corpse holding on to her leg?"

Garrett took a closer look. "Yeah. The body must have frozen—holy *fraxx*. Someone shot the hell out of the body." Now he was paying attention he could see the scorch marks and chunks of missing flesh. Only it wasn't flesh.

"It's a synthetic! Be careful, it might still be active."

And it had a hold of Phylomenia.

He abandoned his plan of approaching slowly. He needed to get to her now and get that thing away from her.

He braced himself for the worst but then gave a whoop of pure joy and relief when she opened her eyes and smiled at him. She was alive.

He didn't slow as he approached, and she opened her arms and prepared to latch on to him.

The second he had her in his arms, he pressed his helmet to hers and yelled, hoping the sound would carry. "You okay?"

Her laugh was the best sound in the whole damned universe. "I'm adrift, low on oxygen, and I have a dead AI frozen to my leg. Fine might be pushing it!"

"Do you have her? Is she okay?" Scott demanded.

"Yes and yes. And apparently that body is not a body. It's an AI."

Scott swore. "Be there in three seconds. Going to try and get that thing off her leg."

"Scott's here!" he shouted to Phylomenia.

She nodded without saying anything more, but her smile widened.

It was the work of just a few minutes to get her untangled from the frozen body of the synthetic, check her suit for damage, and get her set up with a spare air tank.

It still wasn't possible to talk to her without helmet-to-helmet contact, but they were together again.

Garrett refastened their tether lines. Something was deeply satisfying about binding them together this way. It was a safety measure, but the symbolism was deeper than that. This was what he wanted. The three of them linked forever.

When they got back to safety, he'd find a way to make that happen.

They'd only been underway a few minutes when an IAF ship appeared and made its way toward them.

"Did you call for a ride?" Garrett asked.

"I did. Wasn't sure anyone was going to obey orders from me, but it looks like at least some of them didn't buy Halverson's bullshit," Scott replied.

"I guess this means we don't need to figure out how to get back inside a powered down station now. I wasn't sure how that was going to work. This is easier." He reached past Phylomenia to smack Scott on the shoulder, an action that did nothing useful and sent all three of them spinning slowly. "You should have told me about our ride."

"That was my last secret."

"Good. Because I'm not marrying someone who keeps secrets from me." That wasn't what he'd intended to say. Hell. He hadn't even really thought about marriage, apart from a vague determination to make things permanent. Apparently his heart had plans of its own.

"Who says we're getting married? Also, who says you get to be the one to propose? And maybe we should postpone this conversation until Phyl can hear us."

Since his heart had already made its decision, Garrett decided not to fight the inevitable. "I say we're getting married. You have until we get back to bed to decide on your answer, but it better be yes. Then we'll tell our spitfire."

"We're *telling* her?"

"Yup. Telling. I'm not losing either one of you again."

"And if she says no?"

"Anyone who says no is going to stay cuffed to the bed until they make the correct decision. Choose wisely."

To Garrett's joy, Scott laughed. "Now I'm tempted to decline just to spite you."

"Oh, please do."

There was nothing he'd like better than to show his lovers just how far he'd go to keep them together. Now, and forever more.

17

BLADE, LANCE, AND DIRK WERE WAITING AT THE airlock when she stepped off. The identical triplets were all carrying enough weapons to start a small war, and their faces were expressionless masks that kept even the most decorated of Scott's soldiers a safe distance away.

"You here to escort us back to the Nova Club?" she asked.

"We are." Blade glowered at the crowd forming around them. "And to make sure none of these fine folks get it into their heads to do something regrettable, like try and take Colonel Archer into custody."

"We're with him!" someone called.

"Halverson was an ass. What do you want us to do, sir?"

Archer squared his shoulders and stepped forward.

"Continue following my last orders. Get all the civilians you can find to shelter—either the Nova Club or the fleet. If they're VIPs, tell them to return to their hotels or their ships. And under no circumstance is anyone to try and leave this station until we figure out what to do about the nano-swarm currently surrounding this station."

"Sir? What nano-swarm? Is that what happened to the *Victory Dance*?"

"It is. It's also jamming all communications. We'll get it handled. Do your duty. More orders will be coming soon."

After that, he relaxed again, switching from the man she thought of as Archer back to the version of him she liked best—Scotty.

"We, uh, acquired a couple of those self-driving carts. They're down in the maintenance tunnels," Lance said.

"Not taking us through the main areas?" Garrett asked.

"Not this time. And when you do go that way, we'll be coming with you. We're your bodyguards for the time being," Dirk said.

"And if we decline?" Scott asked.

Lance folded his arms over his chest. "It's not your choice to make. We'll tell you when we think it's safe."

Scott and Garrett started to grumble, but Phylomenia took them both by the hand and then smiled at their escort. "Thank you. I've had enough danger for one day."

Even having been told they were all okay, Phylomenia didn't take a proper breath until she had the sprites in her arms and could see for herself that everyone she cared about was safe and well.

"You should have gone to the fleet. What if I hadn't stopped Absalom and that AI bitch in time?" she scolded Zura as she pressed soft kisses to the tops of the twins' heads.

"Chance said we'd be safer here, so we stayed. And you don't get to lecture me on safe choices when you went after Vivian and the Grays alone! What the *fraxx* were you thinking?" Zura shot back.

"That if I didn't stop them, they'd take away everything that mattered to me. You would have done the same." Phylomenia arched a brow at the daughter of her heart. "In fact, I recall you *have* done the same. Going off to save Royan."

"I brought Kit and Luke."

"And I had Gar and Scotty. They just needed to get a few things along the way."

"Like a ship so they could reach you?"

"Well, yes. And what were you thinking, giving them the *Beacon*?"

"I didn't know they'd crash it! There's no traffic out there. They had to deliberately pick the only other ship in the area and steer toward it."

"Mhmm. And that's not the first time they've done

it, either. You are a beautiful, wonderful woman, but, you, my dear, are a lousy judge of character."

"Yet you're the one claiming they're your guys. Don't think I didn't notice that."

"Oh, we're hers." Garrett appeared at her side, his arm slipping around her waist.

"And she's *ours*," Scott declared.

Zura beamed. "Good." She gathered her children back, settling one on each hip. "I can't talk much longer. I need to get the girls back upstairs and then lend a hand around here. Anyone who doesn't trust the IAF seems to have wound up coming here. Alyson and Lieksa have turned the gym into an emergency ward. Serious cases get sent to the med-clinic. Everyone else is just bedding down where they can find room.

"Do you need my room? We've got other places we can go," Phylomenia offered.

"And once I've got things settled back at the base, I'll tell our quartermasters to break out the emergency supplies. Bedding, food. Water. First-aid kits. You should have it all inside an hour," Scott said. "I might not hold this rank for long, but for now, I'm still in charge."

Zura looked torn. "We could use the space, but I don't want you to go."

"This is still my home. I won't be far away."

"Right." Zura looked around, her face solemn. "But I don't know how long this place will be our home. It's not looking good. They still haven't got the main power running. Entire sections of the docking rings are gone. There are minor stress fractures and leaks all over. Royan says we can probably keep this station running for a while, but its days are numbered. Especially if we can't call for help... or leave."

"We'll figure out a way to get past the nano-swarm. Without Absalom or that Vivian-VIDA thing around to control it, it's probably running a basic, reactive program." Phylomenia did her best to sound confident.

The three of them had discussed that on the short ride back to Astek. Once she'd kissed them both breathless of course.

"Vivian. She was really here?" Zura asked.

"Vivian, VIDA, whatever you want to call it. Yeah, it was here in the synthetic flesh. Good thing I'd damaged it enough that the cold of deep space froze it solid before it could do anything more than grab hold of me.

It would be a long time before she'd be able to forget the terrifying moment that thing had caught her as they both tumbled through space. Even once she realized Vivian had frozen solid and was not a threat, she'd been stuck looking at the thing's twisted features, stuck forever in a silent scream.

She shuddered.

"Time to go, spitfire. I believe I promised you a massage," Garrett said.

She leaned into his side. "That sounds like the best plan I've heard all day."

"Where?"

"My place. I need to do some work before I can join you, but I want you both nearby." It was the first time Scott had offered—another sign things were changing. It made her heart happy.

"And the hotel level will be full of petulant, panicky VIPs looking for someone to tell them what's happening so they can yell at them. I'd rather not be the one they descend on," Garrett agreed.

"Call me if you need me," Phyl told Zura but then frowned. "Dammit, I don't have my comm unit anymore."

"Oh, right! Garrett left it with me. I'll have one of the guys meet you by the door with it." Zura grinned. "He must love you. He lugged it all over the station. That thing weighs a ton!"

"I do indeed." Garrett kissed her cheek.

"We'll be back later to help."

"Take your time. You've already done enough for today. Or tonight." Zura's brow furrowed. "Or is it tomorrow already? *Fraxx*. I really need to get the twins to bed and then track down some coffee."

"Coffee sounds good. And food. Also a shower."

"They told us on the way in that the IAF area has partial power. You'll get everything you need and so will everyone here. I'll make sure my engineers are coordinating with Tianna's so we can get the station running as quickly as possible."

They said quick goodbyes to everyone, and

Phylomenia got a hug from Luke along with the return of her battered old comm unit. Something else was in the bag, too, but she kept it to herself for now.

"Thank you," she mouthed the words to Luke. He winked at her and sent them on their way with their three cyborg bodyguards as escorts.

The main concourse looked strange. More emergency lighting had been set up here and there in a mismatch of sizes and colors that bathed the area in weird shades and distorted shadows. The normally packed space was almost empty, though pockets of beings were huddled together in some spots and many of the stores were full of people who watched with blank, unseeing stares, lost in their own trauma and barely aware of anything else.

"Do we know how many?" Phylomenia asked, not wanting to say the last word aloud.

How many *dead*.

"At least a hundred. Likely more. It's impossible to know how many crews were on their ships when the attack started. It looks like most of the locals survived, though. That's something," Scott said.

"It is."

They reached the security check point and their escort left them to return to the club. The check point was manned by a single soldier who looked exhausted but determined. "Sir! Good to see you, sir!" the young man snapped to attention and saluted Scott.

"As you were, Private." Scott leaned in to read his

nametag. "Private Reddy. Are you the same Reddy who got into a bit of trouble defending one of the locals the other day, Private?"

"Uh, yes, sir. That was me. You... you know about that?"

"I know everything that goes on around here, Private. Especially when one of mine goes above and beyond. You risked a fair bit to stand up for what was right. Well done. Is the female and her family safe?"

The lad almost glowed with pride. "Yes, sir! They're with the fleet already, safe and sound. Thank you, sir!"

They were out of earshot before Garrett burst out laughing and then did a dramatic impersonation of Scott. "I know everything that goes on here, Private,"

"Hush, you. I'm a big bad colonel with eyes and ears everywhere. You should fear me," Scott said.

"Ha. You're a sexy as *fraxx* silver fox who better hurry back to us or he's going to get punished," Garrett warned, using that tone that made Phylomenia tingle all the way to her toes.

"Ass," Scott retorted.

"Only if you're on time."

Scott blushed. Actually blushed. But then he turned, caught Garrett by the front of his shirt, and hauled him in for a kiss that should have melted a hole in the floor.

Garrett curled one hand in Scott's hair and reached out to her with the other, pulling her into the middle of their embrace. Kisses and laughter and a few whispered endearments later, they broke apart again.

"I'll take you to my quarters and then leave you to get settled. I'll be back as soon as I can." He shot Garrett a look hotter than the sun. "Don't start without me."

"Start what?" she asked. "I was promised a massage and a shower, no waiting."

Neither man spoke the rest of the walk to Scott's place. They were up to something... and she couldn't wait to find out what it was. Something had changed over the course of the day. It wasn't just the near-death experiences and adrenaline. It was deeper. Stronger.

At least, that's what she wanted it to be.

Scott issued orders, directed supplies and got the ball rolling on a dozen projects to ensure the station and everyone in it survived for the next few days. He instructed everyone to continue to pass the word that no one was to try and leave the station until the barrier was down.

After an hour, he rose from his desk and stretched. He'd been on his feet for the better part of a day now, and even with medi-bots in his system, he was starting to feel the strain. He hadn't eaten or slept properly in far too long. He needed to go home for a few hours.

"Sir?" He'd left his door open, so the newest arrival walked in without waiting for an invitation.

"Commander Kincaid. Glad to see you. How are things looking out there?"

The redheaded engineer shook his head. "Messy. Nothing dire, though. We can slap enough bandages on this thing to keep it airtight and livable for now." He eyed him. "Permission to speak candidly?"

"Granted."

"You look like you're a day late to your own funeral. Get some rest, sir. We've got this handled. If anything blows up or that nano-swarm so much as twitches, I'll let you know."

"Been a busy day."

Kincaid scratched at his beard. "I heard. Got yourself blown up, crashed a ship you didn't own, and had to call for a ride back to the station before you ran out of air."

"All in the line of duty."

"Some days duty is a pain in the asteroid."

"Truer words have not been spoken." Scott nodded. "Send a runner to my quarters if anything looks even the slightest bit strange."

"Yes, sir. See you in a few hours."

Scott didn't wait around. If he did, someone else would come looking for answers or orders. Everyone knew what they needed to do. The gears were moving. Kincaid and the others could manage for a few hours.

He had somewhere else he needed to be.

It was a short walk to his quarters, but by the time he got there some of the weariness had lifted. It wasn't the medi-bots or the coffee he'd consumed. It was because he was about to see his lovers again.

No, not lovers. *Spouses.* At least, that's what they could be if Garrett meant what he'd said earlier.

Scott snorted at his attempt at self-delusion. Garrett meant every word. The question was, was that what *he* wanted?

The answer was an unequivocal *yes*.

He'd spent the better part of a lifetime trying to live up to everyone else's expectation. He was going to take the next few hundred years to discover what he wanted out of life. On the top of his list was Phylomenia and Garrett.

The doors were all on manual, which meant he had to physically pull it open using a handle that had probably never seen use until today.

A soft moan of pleasure greeted him, and he scanned the dimly lit room for the source.

Phylomenia was ensconced in a nest of blankets and pillows, her naked body languid and relaxed. Garrett kneeled beside her, massaging her neck and shoulders. His powerful body was painted by the golden glow of more than a dozen light cubes. Scott allowed himself a moment to enjoy the view before clearing his throat.

"Is this a private spa or can anyone offer their services?"

"I'm all for more servicing." Phyl turned her head and cracked one eye open. "Hey, Scotty. I thought you'd be gone for what's left of the night."

He stripped out of his clothes, tossing them onto the floor for the servo-droids to deal with. "I told you I'd be an hour, and I meant it. My people know what they're doing. I just needed to put things in motion. They can handle it from here."

Garrett nodded toward Phylomenia's feet.

Scott started to obey and then paused long enough to flip his lover off in defiance before taking a seat on the opposite side as Garrett and drawing her legs into his lap.

The bruises were fading already, but he could still see the handprint where that thing had latched on to her leg.

"You should have told us you were banged up," he said, gently lifting one foot and smoothing his hands over the curve of her instep.

"Medi-bots are dealing with the worst of it. A hot shower and some time with both your magic hands will fix the rest." She moaned again as Garrett ran his hands up the sides of her neck.

Scott leaned across her to dip his hands into the bowl of oil Garrett was using. "Where'd you find this?"

"It's olive oil. I had to improvise. You still live like we're just out of basic with nothing to our name but our uniforms."

Scott kept massaging Phyl's foot, his head down so

he didn't have to see the smirk on Garrett's face. "All my good stuff is on the *Bat*. That's my ship, the *Bat Out of Hell*."

"Ah... so you traded your footlocker in for a private starship? I take it back. We *never* lived like that back in the day."

Phylomenia chuckled. "I still don't. In fact, as of this moment, I own about three outfits and a comm unit. The rest is space junk."

"If we could have saved your ship, we would have. Gar's going to buy you a new one, though. Right, Gar?"

"If that's what our spitfire wants." Garrett leaned over to kiss her cheek. "But there's something we need to discuss first. Scott, if you would?"

Scott didn't hesitate. As quickly and gently as he could, he lifted Phylomenia off the floor and onto his lap, still face down.

"Hey! What happened to my massage?"

"Business before pleasure," Garrett almost purred the words as he moved into position across from him.

"I know that tone... and the answer is no. Nope. Not happening. No consent giving. I'm declaring this a no discipline zone." She wriggled and squirmed in Scott's lap, but given her body was covered in oil, all she accomplished was to make his cock harder and smear his legs with oil. He raised his knees just enough to make it impossible for her to pull away, keeping one hand between her shoulder blades.

He and Garrett locked gazes and grinned. She was protesting, but she hadn't used her safe word.

"Mena, you knew this was coming."

"Is this about me leaving you behind? You know I had to do—"

Garrett's hand snapped down, connecting with her right cheek with a satisfying *smack*.

"I had to do it! It was the only way to make sure you and Scotty protected my family."

"You ran, Mena mine. Again." *Smack*.

"But this time you knew where to find me. It's not the same."

The next swat landed on her other cheek, bringing it to the same pink shade as the first one. "You ran from us. That isn't going to happen again."

"Tell him he's right," Scott prompted her, sliding his oiled fingers up the inside of her thigh until his fingertips were grazing the outer lips of her pussy. "Say you're never going to run from us again and we can make you feel better."

"Spank me one more time and I might consider running away *now*," she huffed.

"Wrong answer, spitfire." He withdrew his hand and Garrett swatted her again.

"Jerks! You both suck vacuum." She was squirming again, but she was trying to get closer to his hand, not escape.

He ran his hand up her thigh again, this time pressing the tips of his fingers into her folds the slightest bit before he stopped. "Say it. Say you won't leave us behind again. From now on, whatever comes for us, we face it together."

He moved his fingers a little deeper. "You know what I'd like to be doing right now. Don't make us wait any longer."

Phylomenia moaned. "Alright. Yes. Together. No more running. And that goes for both of you, too."

"That's our girl," Garrett murmured. He stroked Phylomenia's hair and then nodded to Scott. "Give her what she needs."

Scott slid his fingers deeper and was rewarded with a low, needy gasp. "Open for me, Phyl."

She bowed her head and opened her thighs as he lowered his legs back to the floor, giving her more room. He didn't need her submission often, but she seemed to understand his need tonight, and gave him exactly what he wanted.

So did Garrett. He kept one hand on Phylomenia's head and fisted his cock with the other. Thighs spread, stomach taut, his big hand worked the shaft with long, slow strokes.

Phylomenia hummed in approval, her eyes on Garrett.

His cock throbbed as he watched his lovers interacting this way. It was perfect.

"Good girl," he leaned down and kissed her reddened cheek and then rewarded her the best way he could, fucking her with his fingers and working her clit until she was moaning and shuddering in his lap.

"Please. Scotty. I—I need..."

"Say it, spitfire. Tell me what you need and I'll give it to you."

She turned her head and shot him a look that made him laugh out loud.

"Gar? If you would?"

Garrett slapped her ass again. "What do you want, Mena?"

Her body gripped his fingers tightly and a fresh flood of arousal covered his hand.

"I need to come, dammit. One of you make that happen."

"With pleasure." It was the only warning he gave her. His movements sped up and grew stronger, pushing her to the brink and then past it.

Watching her come was one of his favorite sights in the world. He'd never forgotten her passion or her wild ways, and now he'd never have to go without them again.

Garrett met his gaze and smiled. "Guess it's time to finish that conversation from earlier because there isn't a chance in hell I'm letting either of you go now."

"What conversation?" Phylomenia asked.

"The one that involves the only time in his life Gar will kneel for anyone." Scott withdrew his hand and then gently eased her off his lap and back onto the pillows.

"Wait. You're talking about *that* conversation?"

"It was his idea." Scott jerked his head toward Garrett. "Mid-rescue. While you couldn't hear us."

"Did you say no?"

Garrett laughed. "I told him he had until you could hear us to decide."

Phyl sat back, weight on her arms, and looked at the two of them. "So…"

"We're getting married. Soon. You. Me. Scotty. Equal partners for the rest of our lives."

Scott barked out a raw laugh. "Well, that was about as romantic as a three-day march. Did you even read the dating advice book the guys gave us?"

Phylomenia's brows shot up. "Holy *fraxx*. There really is a book? Where? I need to see this!"

"Don't you dare move, spitfire. Yes, there's a book. No, you can't see it right now. And I'm still waiting for your answer." Garrett's voice was pure dominance, and it was the sexiest thing Scott had ever heard.

Phyl tried to hide the little shiver at his tone, but they all saw it. "I don't recall you asking a question. If you want one, try asking me something." Her eyes gleamed. "On your knees."

"This is your fault, Scotty. You just had to mention kneeling." Garrett got to his knees while Scott did the same, arranging themselves so they were kneeling in front of her.

"I told you telling her wouldn't work…"

"Boys. Now is not the time to bicker. Now is the

time for begging." She was grinning as she said it, the little minx.

"We're not begging," Scott started.

"We're asking you to marry us. Please."

"And I'm asking Garrett to marry me, too," Scott added.

Phylomenia clapped. Garrett growled.

"Ha! Too slow. I asked first." Scott chortled and reached out to both of them. "So, are we getting married? I have it on good authority that our answer better be yes."

"Yes," Garrett said, taking his hand.

"Yes," Phylomenia added and then took both their hands.

"Hell yes," Scott said and pulled them both in for a kiss. This was his new life, right here. This man and this woman, his. Forever.

Hands and lips, mouths and tongues, their celebratory kiss quickly ignited into something far more carnal.

Garrett sucked on his fingers. The ones that had been inside Phylomenia a few minutes before. "Want you both. Now."

"Yes," Scott agreed.

"Not just yet. There's something else we need to talk about." Phyl pulled away from them, diving among the pillows and sending some of them flying. "I left it here somewhere. Dammit. Where?"

Both men looked at each other. "Are we losing our touch?" Garrett asked.

"Nope. She's lost her mind. You're still sexy as hell." He caught Garrett by the back of the neck and kissed him while their third rooted through the blankets for another minute.

"Aha! Gotcha," she held up something in triumph, but the light was too dim to make out what it was.

"Yes, you do," Garrett growled as he rocked his cock against Scott's fingers.

"My objective was easier to find than hers... whatever it is."

"This? This is another question." Phylomenia scrambled back to them and held up a slender silver cylinder. "Just how long do you want to stay married to us, Gar-Bear?"

Scott realized what she was holding even as she asked the question. He didn't know where, when, or how, but she'd gotten her hands on another dose of the medi-bots.

"Forever sounds about right," Garrett said.

"I can't promise forever, but how do a few hundred years sound?"

"It sounds like you have more contraband in your possession." Garrett took the injector and stared at it. "So that's it?"

"One shot and you're stuck with us for centuries," Phylomenia said. "You game?"

"Hell yes." Garrett turned to Scott. "Will you?"

"Shoot you full of tiny robots that will let you eat all the ice cream you want for the rest of your life? You know it."

He took the injector and activated it before setting it down nearby. Then he stretched out along one side of their makeshift bed. "I wasn't aware I owned this many pillows."

"You didn't. We raided supply. Now hush. I have a plan." Phyl settled in on her side and then patted the empty spot behind her. "Come here, Gar."

"Ah... I see the plan." Scott rolled onto his side so he was facing her. "You want to be in the middle?"

"Always."

She snuggled in close, letting him draw one of her legs over his so she was open to them both.

His lips found hers, his hands stroking over her body. Her skin was softer than he remembered, her curves lusher, and every inch of her more desirable than the girl in his memories.

"I love you," he whispered before kissing her deeply, drinking her in and letting her oil-slick skin glide over his.

Garrett joined in, the kiss evolving into something messy and sensual, shared between the three of them.

It was perfect.

Scott picked up the injector and then raised his head just enough to be able to see what he was doing. "Forever," he said as he pressed it to Garrett's neck.

"Forever," Phyl echoed.

"That's what I want," Garrett said. "Do it."

"Bossy asshole." Scott pressed the button. After a soft hiss, it was done.

"So, I'm immortal now?" Garrett asked.

"Nope. Not immortal. Next best thing, though. By tomorrow you can say goodbye to all those random aches and pains you've collected over the years," Phyl said, turning her head to kiss Garrett. "And a whole lot more stamina. Lucky, lucky me."

"You have a complaint about my current performance?" Garrett asked and then growled and did something with his hand that made Phylomenia gasp and melt into their arms.

"My only complaint is that there's no performance at the moment." Her voice dropped to a sultry whisper. "I need you both. Now."

"Now that's an order I'm more than happy to comply with." Scott kissed her again, capturing her next moan as a hum against his tongue as it twined with hers. She reached between them, long fingers wrapping around his cock and positioning him so he could claim her with a rock of his hips.

He kept kissing her, hungrily and eagerly, their tongues dancing as her breasts pressed against his chest, her nipples as hard as diamonds.

He entered her slowly, teasing them both by drawing out the moment. Behind her, Garrett shifted, and whatever he did made Phylomenia's body tense around Scott's cock.

"Whatever you did, do it again," he told Garrett.

"Yes. Please. More of that," she murmured, arching first one way and then the other, as if she couldn't decide what she needed more.

He felt the moment Garrett entered her fully. Phyl's moans grew louder, her body stiffening for a moment before relaxing again. Her eyes closed, dark lashes fanning her cheeks as she surrendered herself to them both.

Garrett's eyes burned with need as he eased himself into her, his face a mask of ecstasy. Eyes locked on each other, they linked their hands, using the leverage to increase the depth of their thrusts as they made love to Phylomenia.

Back and forth, one giving way to the other, all three of them connected so intimately it was indescribable. The pleasure built, Garrett's fingers tightening around his as Phylomenia moaned and moved between them. They took their time, wanting to stay in the moment as long as possible, but the better it got, the more his control frayed. Every touch and kiss pushed him closer to the edge.

Phylomenia broke first, and the exquisite grip of her body around his cock snapped the last threads of his control. Pleasure tore through him and he came hard with Garrett only a second behind him.

They stayed locked together for a long time, none of them moving more than they needed to—the brush of a hand, a soft kiss, the touch of a foot to a bare leg.

They drifted together, and for the first time in his life, Scott was at peace. This was what he'd been missing all these years. If this was what the rest of his life would be like, he was ready to move on.

Phylomenia's hand settled on top of their still-clasped fingers, and at the same time they all said the same thing. "I love you."

EPILOGUE

"I guess we'll see you when you get to Haven." Tears shimmered in Zura's silver eyes as she gave Phylomenia one last hug.

"Of course you will. We'll be a few weeks behind you. That's all. We've got to deal with a few things first."

"He'll be okay? They're not actually going to court martial him for saving everyone?" Zura glanced over at Scott, who was saying his own goodbyes to the handful of IAF personnel who had come to see him off. Atun and Ma'ti, the two Pheran street vendors, had come to say farewell, too. They'd brought a basket of *sheka* and fresh *toral* loaf for the trip.

Phylomenia hadn't known about it until later, but Scott had sent soldiers to find the couple and make sure they had everything they needed. He'd been their first customer once the power was back on, too.

Phylomenia lowered her voice. "They've given him the option to retire instead. He's accepted."

"It's already done?"

"In all but name. He's going to retire after this mission. He'll leave with his honor and his pension. They can't take the medi-bots out of his system, so he gets to keep those, too. This is his last act as an IAF officer. He wants to make sure his niece is safe. Then, we'll be coming to Haven."

"And you're all okay with this?"

"More than. The military was a big reason why we broke up the last time. This time, it won't be a factor." Garrett had put in for his retirement, too. Both men would be donating their pensions to a yet-to-be-named nonprofit created by Tianna and some other decent corporate owners to make sure every resident of Astek had everything they needed until the new station was ready.

At least that part of the Grays' plan had failed. Their attempts to trigger some sort of class war had backfired. The beings here and all across the Drift were getting much-needed support, and the Grays were finally being treated as the real threat.

Zura's expression softened. "I admit. I'm looking forward to visiting the new colony. Phaedra can't wait to see us. I want to see Denz and Shadow and meet their new husband. It'll be the first time the girls breathe natural atmosphere."

"I can't wait to see everyone, either. It'll be a nice holiday."

"And then we'll be coming back here." Zura looked around. "Well, not here. But the new station. Tianna won't tell me how much it's costing her to rush the job, but I imagine she could have bought a planet or two and saved herself some money."

The news was out now. Two new stations—one to replace Astek and the other a military base. Tianna had made another announcement, too. The new station wouldn't be run by her company. She'd lease space like everyone else, and a board of governors would be elected to run the day-to-day operations. It would be more than a station. It would represent something new —an unallied, democratic city-state.

"Does the new place have a name yet? I have a bet on it," she asked. She'd been too busy the last few days to keep up with the rapidly changing news.

Zura laughed. "Of course you do. The residents all voted. It's going to be called Defiance."

Phyl crowed. "Ha! I knew it. Your brother owes me big time. Tell him I'll be back to collect my winnings. He's staying here. Isn't he?"

"Tianna won't leave until everyone is safely transferred to the new station and this one is decommissioned. They'll be with her every step of the way." Zura patted the nearest wall. "I'm going to miss this place. It wasn't much, but it was home, you know?"

"No, girl. This is just a place." Phylomenia nodded at Kit and Luke, who were standing not far away with their twin girls in their arms. "That's your home right there."

"Does this mean yours is with them now?" Zura's gaze dropped to the simple gold ring adorning Phylomenia's left ring finger.

She touched the ring and smiled. They'd gotten married last night. It had been the final act of a party celebrating the return to full power for the entire station. Somehow, they'd ended up packed into the *Sun Sprite's* cargo bay with Zura acting as captain of the ship for the ceremony.

Scott had produced rings, Garrett had written up vows, and both of them had grinned like fools the whole time.

Veth, she loved them.

"My home is with them, but you're my family. So I'm going to let you in on a secret." Phyl winked and leaned in close, well aware that no matter what, Zura's husbands would hear every word she said.

"We're coming back. Tianna wants the best security money can buy for the new station. As it happens, I'm married to two of them."

"Yeah? Really!" Zura beamed, her stripes darkening with pleasure. "And what are you going to do while they're keeping us safe?"

"Me? I'm consulting. They might know all there is to know about corporate and military crap, but they don't know a damned thing about the mundane world of criminal enterprise. That happens to be my area of expertise."

"Is that your way of telling me you're quitting?" Zura teased.

"My ship is scrap metal. I'm taking that as a sign it's time for a career change. Besides, for the next while you and Tianna are going to be swamped with freighter jockeys looking for contract work out to the Drift. This place is going to be transformed in the next few months, and where there's money to be made..."

"There will always be pilots looking for their share," Zura finished the quote.

"Not sure they'll come, though. What if the Grays send out another nano-swarm?"

"They won't catch us off guard again. We know what to look for now, and those little bastards died fast once we started using directional EMP blasts on them."

"Yes, they did." Scott joined the conversation. "It was nice to see something go according to plan for once."

"Hey, handsome husband of mine. You almost ready to start your vacation?"

"I am." He gave her a warm smile that melted her heart. "It's been a long time coming."

"You're going to take care of her for me, right?" Zura asked.

Scott tapped his heart. "You have my word. Thanks to Bobbi and Nova Force, we have confirmation that VIDA is Vivian, and that she's capable of splitting herself into different bodies. Absalom might be gone for good... but we can't be sure. Everyone is going to have to watch their backs."

They'd found Absalom's body in the wreckage. Or rather, they'd found the cloned body he'd been using to pass himself off as Verner Lange. The real Lange was still missing, and no one expected to find his body.

Garrett wandered over, accompanied by Chance and Erik. "We ready?" he asked.

"We are," she said.

"Not quite yet," Chance said softly.

Scott slung an arm around both her and Garrett and then looked at Chance. "You're ready to tell us the rest?"

The pretty little cyborg with the almost mystical power of calculation nodded. "I am."

Conversations died away as everyone focused their attention on Chance.

"And?" Zura prompted.

"This is only the ending of a chapter, not the story. We'll see each other again." Chance's smile lit up the room. "The adventure will continue."

Phylomenia took a moment to soak it all in. Family. Friends. New dreams and her new husbands. She had so much more than she'd ever dared to dream of.

Then she slapped both her men on the ass and

grinned. "Damned right this story will continue. And it starts with the words 'they lived happily ever after.'"

Thank You for Reading Winner Takes All!

I hope you enjoyed Phyl, Scott, and Garrett's story. If you're looking for more stories like this one, I invite you to explore the other books in the Drift universe, which include both the Nova Force and Haven Colony series.

ABOUT THE AUTHOR

Susan lives out on the Canadian west coast surrounded by open water, dear family, and good friends. She's jumped out of perfectly good airplanes on purpose and accidentally swum with sharks on the Great Barrier Reef.

If the world ends, she plans to survive as the spunky, comedic sidekick to the heroes of the new world, because she's too damned short and out of shape to make it on her own for long.

You can find out more about Susan and her books at:
www.susanhayes.ca